The Hohenzollerns in America

Stephen Leacock

Contents

I.--The Hohenzollerns in America 7

II.--With the Bolsheviks in Berlin..40

III.--Afternoon Tea with the Sultan 53

IV.--Echoes of the War 60

V.--Other Impossibilities..91

THE HOHENZOLLERNS IN AMERICA

BY

Stephen Leacock

I.--The Hohenzollerns in America

PREFACE

The proper punishment for the Hohenzollerns, and the Hapsburgs, and the Mecklenburgs, and the Muckendorfs, and all such puppets and princelings, is that they should be made to work; and not made to work in the glittering and glorious sense, as generals and chiefs of staff, and legislators, and land-barons, but in the plain and humble part of laborers looking for a job; that they should carry a hod and wield a trowel and swing a pick and, at the day's end, be glad of a humble supper and a night's rest; that they should work, in short, as millions of poor emigrants out of Germany have worked for generations past; that there should be about them none of the prestige of fallen grandeur; that, if it were possible, by some trick of magic, or change of circumstance, the world should know them only as laboring men, with the dignity and divinity of kingship departed out of them; that, as such, they should stand or fall, live or starve, as best they might by the work of their own hands and brains. Could this be done, the world would have a better idea of the thin stuff out of which autocratic kingship is fashioned.

It is a favourite fancy of mine to imagine this transformation actually brought about; and to picture the Hohenzollerns as an immigrant family departing for America, their trunks and boxes on their backs, their bundles in their hands.

The fragments of a diary that here follow present the details of such a picture. It is written, or imagined to be written, by the (former) Princess Frederica of Hohenzollern. I do not find her name in the Almanach de Gotha. Perhaps she does not exist. But from the text below she is to be presumed to be one of the innumerable nieces of the German Emperor.

CHAPTER I

On Board the S.S. America. Wednesday

At last our embarkation is over, and we are at sea. I am so glad it is done. It was dreadful to see poor Uncle William and Uncle Henry and Cousin Willie and Cousin Ferdinand of Bulgaria, coming up the gang-plank into the steerage, with their boxes on their backs. They looked so different in their rough clothes. Uncle William is wearing an old blue shirt and a red handkerchief round his neck, and his hair looks thin and unkempt, and his moustache draggled and his face unshaved. His eyes seem watery and wandering, and his little withered arm so pathetic. Is it possible he was always really like that?

At the top of the gang-plank he stood still a minute, his box still on his back, and said, "This then is the pathway to Saint Helena." I heard an officer down on the dock call up, "Now then, my man, move on there smartly, please." And I saw some young roughs pointing at Uncle and laughing and saying, "Look at the old guy with the red handkerchief. Is he batty, eh?"

The forward deck of the steamer, the steerage deck, which is the only place that we are allowed to go, was crowded with people, all poor and with their trunks and boxes and paper bags all round them. When Uncle set down his box, there was soon quite a little crowd around him, so that I could hardly see him. But I could hear them laughing, and I knew that they were "taking a rise out of him," as they call it,--just as they did in the emigration sheds on shore. I heard Uncle say, "Let wine be brought: I am faint;" and some one else said, "Yes, let it," and there arose a big shout of laughter.

Cousin Willie had sneaked away with his box down to the lower deck. I thought it mean of him not to stay with his father. I never noticed till now what a sneaking face Cousin Willie has. In his uniform, as Crown Prince, it was different. But in his shabby clothes, among these rough people, he seems so changed. He walks with a mean stoop, and his eyes look about in such a furtive way, never still. I saw one of the ship's officers watching him, very closely and sternly.

Cousin Karl of Austria, and Cousin Ruprecht of Bavaria, are not here. We thought they were to come on this ship, but they are not here. We could hardly believe that the ship would sail without them.

I managed to get Uncle William out of the crowd and down below. He was glad to get off the deck. He seemed afraid to look at the sea, and when we got into the big cabin, he clutched at the cover of the port and said, "Shut it, help me shut it, shut out the sound of the sea;" and then for a little time he sat on one of the bunks all hunched up, and muttering, "Don't let me hear the sea, don't let me hear it." His eyes looked so queer and fixed, that I thought he must be in a sort of fit, or seizure. But Uncle Henry and Cousin Willie and Cousin Ferdinand came into the cabin and he got better again.

Cousin Ferdinand has got hold of a queer long overcoat with the sleeves turned up, and a little round hat, and looks exactly like a Jew. He says he traded one of our empty boxes for the coat and hat. I never noticed before how queer and thick Cousin Ferdinand's speech is, and how much he gesticulates with his hands when he talks. I am sure that when I visited at Sofia nobody ever noticed it. And he called Uncle William and Uncle Henry "Mister," and said that on the deck he had met two "fine gentlemen," (that's what he called them), who are in the clothing trade in New York. It was with them he traded for the coat.

Cousin Ferdinand, who is very clever at figures, is going to look after all our money, because the American money is too difficult for Uncle William and Cousin Willie to understand. We have only a little money, but Cousin Ferdinand said that we would put it all together and make it a pool. But when Uncle Henry laughed, and turned his pockets out and had no money at all, Cousin Ferdinand said that it would NOT be a pool. He said he would make it "on shares" and explained it, but I couldn't understand what it meant.

While he was talking I saw Cousin Willie slip one of the pieces of money out of the pile into his pocket: at least I think I saw it; but he did it so quickly that I was not sure, and didn't like to say anything.

Then a bell rang and we went to eat in a big saloon, all crowded with common people, and very stuffy. The food was wretched, and I could not eat. I suppose Uncle was famished from the long waiting and the bad food in the emigrant shed. It was dreadful to see the hungry way that he ate the greasy stew they gave us, with his head down almost in his plate and his moustache all unkempt. "This ragout is admirable," he said. "Let the chef be informed that I said it."

Cousin Ferdinand didn't sit with us. He sat beside his two new friends and they had their heads all close together and talked with great excitement. I never knew before that Cousin Ferdinand talked Yiddish. I remember him at Sofia, on horseback addressing his army, and I don't think he talked to his troops in Yiddish. He was telling them, I remember, how sorry he was that he couldn't accompany them to the front. But for "business in Sofia," he said, he would like to be in the very front trenches, the foremost of all. It was thought very brave of him.

When we got up from supper, the ship was heaving and rolling quite a bit. A young man, a steward, told us that we were now out of the harbor and in the open sea. Uncle William told him to convey his compliments to the captain on his proper navigation of the channel. The young man looked very closely at Uncle and said, "Sure, I'll tell him right away," but he said it kindly. Then he said to me, when Uncle couldn't hear, "Your pa ain't quite right, is he, Miss Hohen?" I didn't know what he meant, but, of course, I said that Uncle William was only my uncle. Hohen is, I should explain, the name by which we are known now. The young man said that he wasn't really a steward, only just for the trip. He said that, because I had a strange feeling that I had met him before, and asked him if I hadn't seen him at one of the courts. But he said he had never been "up before one" in his life. He said he lives in New York, and drives an ice-wagon and is an ice-man. He said he was glad to have the pleasure of our acquaintance. He is, I think, the first ice-man I have ever met. He reminds me very much of the Romanoffs, the Grand Dukes of the younger branch, I mean. But he says he is not connected with them, so far as he knows. He said his name is Peters. We have no Almanach de Gotha here on board the steamer, so I cannot look up his name.

S.S. America. Thursday

We had a dreadful experience last night. In the middle of the night Uncle Henry came and called me and said that Uncle William was ill. So I put on an old shawl and went with him. The ship was pitching and heaving with a dreadful straining and creaking noise. A dim light burned in the cabin, and outside there was a great roaring of the wind and the wild sound of the sea surging against the ship.

Uncle William was half sitting up in his rough bunk, with the tattered gray blankets over him, one hand was clutched on the side of the bed and there was a great horror in his eyes. "The sea; the sea," he kept saying, "don't let me hear it. It's THEIR voices. Listen! They're beating at the sides of the ship. Keep them from me, keep them out!"

He was quiet for a minute, until there came another great rush of the sea against the sides of the ship, and a roar of water against the port. Then he broke out, almost screaming--"Henry, brother Henry, keep them back! Don't let them drag me down. I never willed it. I never wanted it. Their death is not at my door. It was necessity. Henry! Brother Henry! Tell them not to drag me below the sea!"

Like that he raved for perhaps an hour and we tried to quiet him. Cousin Willie had slipped away, I don't know where. Cousin Ferdinand was in his bunk with his back turned.

"Do I slip to-night, at all," he kept growling "or do I not? Say, mister, do I get any slip at all?"

But no one minded him.

Then daylight came and Uncle fell asleep. His face looked drawn and gray and the cords stood out on his withered hand, which was clutched against his shirt.

So he slept. It seemed so strange. There was no court physician, no bulletins to reassure the world that he was sleeping quietly.

Later in the morning I saw the ship's doctor and the captain, all in uniform, with gold braid, walking on their inspection round.

"You had some trouble here last night," I heard the captain say.

"No, nothing," the doctor answered, "only one of the steerage passengers delirious in the night."

Later in the morning the storm had gone down and the sea was calm as glass, and Uncle Henry and I got Uncle William up on deck. Mr. Peters, the steward that I think I spoke about before, got us a steamer chair from the first class that had been thrown away--quite good except for one leg,--and Uncle William sat in it with his face away from the sea. He seemed much shaken and looked gray and tired, but he talked quite quietly and rationally about our going to America, and how we must all work, because work is man's lot. He himself, he says, will take up the presidency of Harvard University in New York, and Uncle Henry, who, of course, was our own Grand Admiral and is a sailor, will enter as Admiral of the navy of one of the states, probably, Uncle says, the navy of Missouri, or else that of Colorado.

It was pleasant to hear Uncle William talk in this way, just as quietly and rationally as at Berlin, and with the same grasp of political things. He only got excited once, and that was when he was telling Uncle Henry that it was his particular wish that Uncle should go to the captain and offer to take over the navigation of the vessel. Uncle Henry is a splendid sailor, and in all our cruises in the Baltic he used to work out all the navigation of the vessel, except, of course, the arithmetic--which was beneath him.

Uncle Henry laughed (he is always so good natured) and said that he had had enough of being Admiral to last him all his life. But when Uncle William insisted, he said he would see what he could do.

S.S. America. Friday

All yesterday and to-day the sea was quite calm, and we could sit on deck. I was glad because, in the cabin where I am, there are three other women, and it is below the water-line, and is very close and horrid. So when it is rough, I can only sit in the alley-way with my knitting. There the light is very dim and the air bad. But I do not complain. It is woman's lot. Uncle William and Cousin Willie have both told me this--that it is woman's lot to bear and to suffer; and they said it with such complete resignation that I feel I ought to imitate their attitude.

Cousin Ferdinand, too, is very brave about the dirt and the discomfort of being on board the ship. He doesn't seem to mind the dirt at all, and his new friends (Mr. Sheehan and Mr. Mosenhammer) seem to bear it so well, too. Uncle Henry goes and washes his hands and face at one of the ship's pumps before every meal, with a great noise and splashing, but Cousin Ferdinand says, "For me the pump, no." He says that nothing like that matters now, and that his only regret is that he did not fall at the head of his troops, as he would have done if he had not been detained by business.

I caught sight of Cousin Karl of Austria! So it seems he is on the ship after all. He was up on the promenade deck where the first class passengers are, and of which you can just see one end from down here in the steerage. Cousin Karl had on a waiter's suit and was bringing something to drink to two men who were in steamer chairs on the deck. I don't know whether he saw me or not, but if he did he didn't give any sign of recognizing me. One of the men gave Cousin Karl a piece of money and I was sure it was he, from the peculiar, cringing way in which he bowed. It was just the manner that he used to have at Vienna with his cousin, Franz Ferdinand, and with dear old Uncle Franz Joseph.

We always thought, we girls I mean, that it was Cousin Karl who had Cousin Franz Ferdinand blown up at Serajevo. I remember once we dared Cousin Zita, Karl's wife, to ask Uncle William if it really was Karl. But Uncle William spoke very gravely, and said that it was not a thing for us to discuss, and that if Karl did it, it was an "act of State," and no doubt very painful to Cousin Karl to have to do. Zita asked Uncle if Karl poisoned dear old Uncle Franz Joseph, because some of Karl's best and most intimate friends said that he did. But Uncle said very positively, "No," that dear old Uncle Franz Joseph had not needed any poison, but had died, very naturally, under the hands of Uncle William's own physician, who was feeling his wind-pipe at the time.

Of course, all these things seem very far away now. But seeing Cousin Karl on the upper deck, reminded me of all the harmless gossip and tattle that used to go on among us girls in the old days.

Friday afternoon

I saw Cousin Willie on the deck this afternoon. I had not seen him all day yesterday as he seems to keep out of sight. His eyes looked bloodshot and I was sure that he had been drinking.

I asked him where he had been in the storm while Uncle William was ill. He gave a queer sort of leering chuckle and said, "Over there," and pointed backwards with his thumb towards the first class part of the ship. Then he said, "Come here a minute," and he led me round a corner to where no one could see, and showed me a gold brooch and two diamond rings. He told me not to tell the others, and then he tried to squeeze my hand and to pull me towards him, in such a horrid way, but I broke away and went back. Since then I have been trying to think how he could have got the brooch and the rings. But I cannot think.

S.S. America. Saturday

To-day when I went up on deck, the first thing I saw was Uncle Henry. I hardly recognized him. He had on an old blue sailor's jersey, and was cleaning up a brass rail with a rag. I asked him why he was dressed like that and Uncle Henry laughed and said he had become an admiral. I couldn't think what he meant, as I never guess things with a double meaning, so he explained that he has got work as a sailor for the voyage across. I thought he looked very nice in his sailor's jersey, much nicer than in the coat with gold facings, when he was our High Admiral. He reminded me very much of those big fair-haired Norwegian sailors that we used to see when we went on the Meteor to Flekkefyord and Gildeskaale. I am sure that he will be of great service to this English captain, in helping to work the ship across.

When Cousin Ferdinand came up on deck with his two friends, Mr. Mosenhammer and Mr. Sheehan, he was very much interested in Uncle Henry's having got work. He made an arrangement right away that he would borrow Uncle Henry's wages, and that Mr. Sheehan would advance them, and he would then add it to our capital, and then he would take it and keep it. Uncle Henry is to get what is called, in the new money, one seventy-five a day, and to get it for four days, and Cousin Ferdinand says that comes to four dollars and a quarter. Cousin Ferdinand is very quick with figures. He says that he will have to take out a small commission for managing the money for Uncle Henry, and that later on he will tell Uncle Henry how much will be left after taking it out. Uncle Henry said all right and went on with his brass work. It is strange how his clothes seem to change him. He looks now just like a rough, common sailor.

S.S. America. Tuesday

To-day our voyage is to end. I am so glad. When we came on deck Mr. Peters told me that we were in sight of land. He told me the names of the places, but they were hard and difficult to remember, like Long Island and Sandy Hook; not a bit like our dear old simple German names.

So we were all told to put our things together and get ready to land. I got, out of one of our boxes, an old frock coat for Uncle William. It is frayed at the ends of the sleeves and it shines a little, but I had stitched it here and there and it looked quite nice. He put it on with a pair of gray trousers that are quite good, and not very much bagged, and I had knitted for him a red necktie that he wears over his blue shirt with a collar, called a celluloid collar, that American gentlemen wear.

The sea is so calm that Uncle doesn't mind being on deck now, and he even came close to the bulwarks, which he wouldn't do all the way across. He stood there in quite an attitude with his imperfect hand folded into his coat. He looked something, but not quite, as he used to look on the deck of the Meteor in the Baltic.

Presently he said, "Henry, your arm!" and walked up and down with Uncle Henry. I could see that the other passengers were quite impressed with the way Uncle looked, and it pleased him. I heard some rough young loafers saying, "Catch on to the old Dutch, will you? Eh, what?"

Uncle Henry is going ashore just as he is, in his blue jersey. But Cousin Ferdinand has put on a bright red tie that Mr. Mosenhammer has loaned to him for three hours.

Cousin Willie only came on deck at the very last minute, and he seemed anxious to slink behind the other passengers and to keep out of sight. I think it must have something to do with the brooch that he showed me, and the rings. His eyes looked very red and bloodshot and his face more crooked and furtive than ever. I am sure that he had been drinking again.

I have written the last lines of this diary sitting on the deck. We have just passed a huge statue that rises out of the water, the name of which they mentioned but I can't remember, as it was not anything I ever heard of before.

Just think--in a little while we shall land in America!

CHAPTER II

City New York. 2nd Avenue
We came off the steamer late yesterday afternoon and came across the city to a pension on Second Avenue where we are now. Only here they don't call it a pension but a boarding house. Cousin Ferdinand and Cousin Willie drove across in the cart with our boxes, and Uncle William and Uncle Henry and I came on a street car. It cost us fifteen cents. A cent is four and one-sixth pfennigs. We tried to reckon what it came to, but we couldn't; but Uncle Henry thinks it could be done.

This house is a tall house in a mean street, crowded and noisy with carts and street-sellers. I think it would be better to have all the boarding houses stand far back from the street with elm trees and fountains and lawns where peacocks could walk up and down. I am sure it would be MUCH better.

We have taken a room for Uncle William and Uncle Henry on the third floor at the back and a small room in the front for me of the kind called a hall bedroom, which I don't ever remember seeing before. There were none at Sans Souci and none, I think, at any of the palaces. Cousin Willie has a room at the top of the house, and Cousin Ferdinand in the basement.

The landlady of this house is very stout and reminds me very much of the Grand Duchess of Sondersburg-Augustenburg: her manner when she showed us the rooms was very like that of the Grand Duchess; only perhaps a little firmer and more authoritative. But it appears that they are probably not related, as the landlady's name is Mrs. O'Halloran, which is, I think, Scotch.

When we arrived it was already time for dinner so we went downstairs to it at once. The dining-room was underground in the basement. It was very crowded and stuffy, and there was a great clatter of dishes and a heavy smell of food. Most of the people were already seated, but there was an empty place at the head of one of the tables and Uncle William moved straight towards that. Uncle was wearing, as I said, his frock coat and his celluloid collar and he walked into the room with quite an air, in something of the way that he used to come into the great hall of the Neues Palais at Potsdam, only that in these clothes it looked different. As Uncle entered the room he waved his hand and said, "Let no one rise!" I remember that when Uncle said this at the big naval dinner at Kiel it made a great sensation as an example of his ready tact. He realised that if they had once risen there would have been great difficulty in their order of procedure for sitting down again. He was afraid that the same difficulty might have been felt here in the boarding house. But I don't think it would, and I don't think that they were going to stand up, anyway. They just went on eating. I noticed one cheap-looking young man watching Uncle with a sort of half smile as he moved towards his seat. I heard him say to his neighbour, "Some scout, eh?"

The food was so plain and so greasy that I could hardly eat it. But I have noticed that it is a strange thing about Uncle that he doesn't seem to know what he eats at all. He takes all this poor stuff that they put before him to be the same delicacies that we had at the Neues Palais and Sans Souci. "Is this a pheasant?" he asked when the servant maid passed him his dish of meat. I heard the mean young man whisper, "I guess not." Presently some hash was brought in and Uncle said, "Ha! A Salmi! Ha! excellent!" I could see that Mrs. O'Halloran, the landlady, who sat at the other end of the table, was greatly pleased.

I was surprised to find--because it is so hard to get used to the change of things in our new life--that all the people went on talking just the same after Uncle sat down. At the palace at Potsdam nobody ever spoke at dinner unless Uncle William first addressed him, and then he was supposed to give a sort of bow and answer as briefly as possible so as not to interrupt the flow of Uncle William's conversation. Generally Uncle talked and all the rest listened. His conversation was agreed by everybody to be wonderful. Princes, admirals, bishops, artists, scholars and everybody united in declaring that Uncle William showed a range of knowledge and a brilliance of language that was little short of marvellous. So naturally it was a little disappointing at first to find that these people just went on talking to one another and didn't listen to Uncle William at all, or merely looked at him in an inquisitive sort of way and whispered remarks to one another. But presently, I don't just know how, Uncle began to get the attention of the table and one after the other the people stopped talking to listen to him. I was very glad of this because Uncle was talking about America and I was sure that it would interest them, as what he said was very much the same as the wonderful speech that he made to the American residents of Berlin at the time when the first exchange professor was sent over to the University. I remember that all the Americans who heard it said that Uncle told them things about their own country that they had never known, or even suspected, before. So I was glad when I heard Uncle explaining to these people the wonderful possibilities of their country. He talked of the great plains of Connecticut and the huge seaports of Pittsburg and Colorado Springs, and the tobacco forests of Idaho till one could just see it all. He said that the Mississippi, which is a great river here as large as the Weser, should be dammed back and held while a war of extermination was carried on against the Indians on the other side of it with a view to Christianizing them. The people listened, their faces flushed with eating and with the close air. Here and there some of them laughed or nudged one another and said, "Get on to this, will you?" But I remember that when Uncle William made this speech in Berlin the Turkish ambassador said after it that he now knew so much about America that he wanted to die, and that the Shah of Persia wrote a letter to Uncle, all in his own writing, except the longest words, and said that he had ordered Uncle's speech on America to be printed and read aloud by all the schoolmasters in Persia under penalty of decapitation. Nearly all of them read it.

Wednesday

This morning we had a great disappointment. It had been pretty well arranged on board the ship that Uncle would take over the presidency of Harvard University. Uncle Henry and Cousin Ferdinand and Cousin Willie had all consented to it, and we looked upon it as done. Now it seems there is a mistake. First of all Harvard University is not in New York, as we had always thought in Germany that it was. I remember that when Uncle Henry came home from his great tour in America, in which he studied American institutions so profoundly, and made his report he said that Harvard University was in New York. Uncle had this information filed away in our Secret Service Department.

But it seems that it is somewhere else. The University here is called Columbia, so Uncle decided that he would be president of that. In the old days all the great men of learning used to assure Uncle that if fate had not made him an emperor he would have been better fitted than any living man to be the head of a great university. Uncle admitted this himself, though he resented being compared only to the living ones.

So it was a great disappointment to-day when they refused to give him the presidency. I went with him to the college, but I cannot quite understand what happened or why they won't give it to him. We walked all the way up and I carried a handbag filled with Uncle's degrees and diplomas from Oxford and all over the world. All the way up Uncle talked about the majesty and the freedom of learning and what he would do to the college when he was made president, and how all the professors should sit up and obey him. At times he got so excited that he would stop on the street and wave his hands and gesticulate so that people turned and looked at him. At Potsdam we never realized that Uncle was excited all the time, and, in any case, with his uniform on and his sabre clattering as he walked, it all seemed different. But here in the street, in his faded frock coat and knitted tie, and with his face flushed and his eyes rambling, people seemed to mistake it and thought that his mind was not quite right.

So I think he made a wrong impression when we went into the offices of the college. Uncle was still quite excited from his talking. "Let the trustees be brought," he said in a peremptory way to the two young men in black frock coats, secretaries of some sort, I suppose, who received us. Then he turned to me. "Princess," he said, "my diplomas!" He began pulling them out of the bag and throwing them on the table in a wild sort of way. The other people waiting in the room were all staring at him. Then the young men took Uncle by the arm and led him into an inner room and I went out into the corridor and waited. Presently one of the young men came out and told me not to wait, as Uncle had been sent home in a cab. He was very civil and showed me where to go to get the elevated railroad. But while I was waiting I had overheard some of the people talking about Uncle. One said, "That's that same old German that was on board our ship last week in the steerage--has megalomania or something of the sort, they say, and thinks he's the former Emperor: I saw the Kaiser once at a review in Berlin,--not much resemblance, is there?"

CHAPTER III

For weeks and weeks I have written nothing in my diary because it has been so discouraging. After Uncle William's offer to take over the presidency of Columbia University had been refused, he debated with Uncle Henry and with Cousin Ferdinand of Bulgaria (who is not living in our boarding house now but who comes over quite often in the evenings) whether he would accept the presidency of Harvard. Cousin Ferdinand looked up the salary in a book and told him not to take it. Cousin Ferdinand has little books with all the salaries of people in America and he says that these books are fine and much better than the Almanach de Gotha which we used to use in Europe to hunt people up. He says that if he ever goes back to be King of Bulgaria again he is going to introduce books like these. Cousin Ferdinand is getting very full of American ideas and he says that what you want to know about a man is not his line of descent but his line of credit. And he says that the whole King business in Europe has been mismanaged. He says that there should have been millions in it. I forgot to say in my diary sooner that Cousin Ferdinand's two friends, Mr. Mosenhammer and Mr. Sheehan, took him into their clothing business at once as a sort of partner. The reason was that they found that he could wear clothes; the effect on the customers when they see Cousin Ferdinand walking up and down in front of the store is wonderful. Of course all kings can wear clothes and in the old days in the Potsdam palace we thought nothing of it. But Cousin Ferdinand says that the kings should have known enough to stop trying to be soldiers and to put themselves at the head of the export clothing trade. He wishes, he says, that he had some of his Bulgarian generals here now in their blue coats trimmed with black fur; he says that with a little alteration, which he showed us how to do, he could have sent them out "on the road," wherever that is, and have made the biggest boom in gentlemen's winter fur trimmings that the trade ever saw.

Cousin Ferdinand, when he comes over in the evenings now, is always beautifully dressed and I can notice that Mrs. O'Halloran, the landlady, is much impressed with him. I am glad of this because we have not yet been able to pay her any money and I was afraid she might say something about it. But what is stranger is that now that Cousin Ferdinand has good clothes, Uncle William and Uncle Henry seem much impressed too. Uncle Henry looks so plain and common in his sailor's jersey, and Uncle William in his old frock coat looks faded and shabby and his face always vacant and wondering. So now when Cousin Ferdinand comes in they stand up and get a chair for him and listen to his advice on everything.

So, as I said, Cousin Ferdinand looked up the salary of the President of Harvard in a book and he was strongly against Uncle William's taking the position. But Uncle William says this kind of position is the nearest thing in this country to what he had in Germany. He thinks that he could do for Harvard what he did for Germany. He has written out on a big sheet of paper all the things that he calls the Chief Needs of America, because he is always busy like this and never still. I forget the whole list, especially as he changes it every day according to the way that people treat Uncle William on the street, but the things that he always puts first are Culture, Religion, and Light. These he says he can supply, and he thought that the presidency of Harvard would be the best place to do it from. In the end he accepted the position against Cousin Ferdinand's advice, or at least I mean he said that he would be willing to take it and he told Uncle Henry to pack up all his degrees and diplomas and to send them to Harvard and say that he was coming.

So it was dreadfully disappointing when all the diplomas came back again by the next post. There was a letter with them but I didn't see it, as Uncle William tore it into fragments and stamped on it. He said he was done with American universities for ever; I have never seen him so furious: he named over on his fingers all the American professors that he had fed at Berlin, one meal each and sometimes even two,--Uncle has a wonderful memory for things like that,--and yet this was their gratitude. He walked up and down his room and talked so wildly and incoherently that if I had not known and been told so often by our greatest authorities in Germany how beautifully balanced Uncle William's brain is, I should have feared that he was wandering.

But presently he quieted down and said with deep earnestness that the American universities must now go to ruin in their own way. He was done with them. He said he would go into a cloister and spend his life in quiet adoration, provided that he could find anything to adore, which, he said, in his station was very doubtful. But half an hour later he was quite cheerful again,--it is wonderful how quickly Uncle William's brain recovers itself,--and said that a cloister was too quiet and that he would take a position as Governor of a State; there are a great many of these in this country and Uncle spent days and days writing letters to them and when the answers came in-- though some never answered at all--Uncle William got into the same state of fury as about the Presidency of Harvard. So, naturally, each day seemed more disappointing than the last, especially with the trouble that we have been having with Cousin Willie, of which I have not spoken yet, and I was getting quite disheartened until last evening, when everything seemed to change.

We all knew, of course, that Uncle William is the greatest artist in the world, but no one liked to suggest that he should sell his pictures for money, a thing that no prince was ever capable of doing. Yet I could not but feel glad when Uncle decided yesterday that he would stoop to make his living by art. It cost him a great struggle to make this decision, but he talked it over very fully last night with Uncle Henry, after Uncle Henry came home from work, and the resolution is taken.

Of course, Uncle always had a wonderful genius for painting. I remember how much his pictures used to be admired at the court at Berlin. I have seen some of the best painters stand absolutely entranced,--they said so themselves,--in front of Uncle's canvasses. I remember one of the greatest of our artists saying one day to Uncle in the Potsdam Gallery, "Now, which of these two pictures is yours and which is Michel Angelo's: I never can tell you two apart." Uncle gave him the order of the Red Swan. Another painter once said that if Uncle's genius had been developed he would have been the greatest painter of modern times. Uncle William, I remember, was dreadfully angry. He said it WAS developed.

So it seemed only natural that Uncle should turn to Art to make our living. But he hesitated because there is some doubt whether a person of noble birth can sell anything for money. But Uncle says Tintoretto the great Italian artist had two quarterings of nobility, and Velasquez had two and a half.

Luckily we have with us among our things Uncle's easel and his paints that he used in Berlin. He had always to have special things because he doesn't use little brushes and tubes of colour as ordinary artists do, but had a big brush and his paint in a tin can, so that he can work more quickly. Fortunately we have with us three of Uncle's pictures rolled up in the bottom of our boxes. He is going to sell these first and after that he says that he will paint one or two every day. One of the three canvasses that we have is an allegorical picture called "Progress" in which Progress is seen coming out of a cloud in the background with Uncle William standing in the foreground. Another is called "Modern Science" and in this Science is seen crouched in the dark in the background and Uncle William standing in the light in the foreground. The other is called "Midnight in the Black Forest." Uncle William did it in five minutes with a pot of black paint. They say it is impressionistic.

So all the evening Uncle William and Uncle Henry talked about the new plan. It is wonderful how Uncle William enters into a thing. He got me to fetch him his old blue blouse, which was with the painting things, and he put it on over his clothes and walked up and down the room with a long paint-brush in his hand. "We painters, my dear Henry," he said, "must not be proud. America needs Art. Very good. She shall have it."

I could see, of course, that Uncle William did not like the idea of selling pictures for money. But he is going to make that side of it less objectionable by painting a picture, a very large picture, for nothing and giving it to the big Metropolitan Art Gallery which is here. Uncle has already partly thought it out. It is to be called the "Spirit of America" and in it the Spirit of America will be seen doubled up in the background: Uncle has not yet fully thought out the foreground, but he says he has an idea.

In any case he is going to refuse to take anything more than a modest price for his pictures. Beyond that, he says, not one pfennig.

So this morning Uncle rolled up his three canvasses under his arm and has gone away to sell them.

I am very glad, as we have but little money, indeed hardly any except Uncle Henry's wages. And I have been so worried, too, and surprised since we came here about Cousin Willie. He hardly is with the rest of us at all. He is out all night and sleeps in the day time, and often I am sure that he has been drinking. One morning when he came back to the house at about breakfast time he showed me quite a handful of money, but wouldn't say where he got it. He said there was lots more where it came from. I asked him to give me some to pay Mrs. O'Halloran, but he only laughed in his leering way and said that he needed it all. At another time when I went up to Cousin Willie's room one day when he was out, I saw quite a lot of silver things hidden in a corner of the cupboard. They looked like goblets and silver dinner things, and there was a revolver and a sheath-knife hidden with them. I began to think that he must have stolen all these things, though it seemed impossible for a prince. I have spoken to Uncle William several times about Cousin Willie, but he gets impatient and does not seem to care. Uncle never desires very much to talk of people other than himself. I think it fatigues his mind. In any case, he says that he has done for Willie already all that he could. He says he had him confined to a fortress three times and that four times he refused to have him in his sight for a month, and that twice he banished him to a country estate for six weeks. His duty, he says, is done. I said that I was afraid that Cousin Willie had been stealing and told him about the silver things hidden in the cupboard. But Uncle got very serious and read me a very severe lecture. No prince, he said, ever stole. His son, he explained, might very well be collecting souvenirs as memorials of his residence in America: all the Hohenzollerns collected souvenirs: some of our most beautiful art things at Potsdam and Sans Souci were souvenirs collected by our ancestors in France fifty years ago. Uncle said that if the Great War had turned out as it should and if his soldiers had not betrayed him by getting killed, we should have had more souvenirs than ever. After that he dismissed the subject from his mind. Uncle William can dismiss things from his mind more quickly than anybody I ever knew.

The Same Day. Later

I was so surprised this afternoon, when I happened to go down to the door, to see Mr. Peters, the ice gentleman that was on the ship, with his ice cart delivering ice into the basement. I knew that he delivered ice in this part of the city because he said so, and I think he had mentioned this street, and two or three times I thought I had seen him from the window. But it did seem surprising to happen to go down to the door (I forget what I went for) at the moment that he was there. He looked very fine in his big rough suit of overalls. It is not quite like a military uniform, but I think it looks better. Mr. Peters knew me at once. "Good afternoon, Miss Hohen," he said (that is the name, as I think I said, that we have here), "how are all the folks?"

So we talked for quite a little time, and I told him about Uncle trying to get work and how hard it was and how at last he had got work, or at least had gone out to get it, as a painter. Mr. Peters said that that was fine. He said that painters do well here: he has a lot of friends who are painters and they get all the way from sixty to seventy-five cents an hour. It seems so odd to think of them being paid by the hour. I don't think the court artists at home were paid like that. It will be very nice if Uncle William can mingle with Mr. Peters's artist friends. Mr. Peters asked if he might take me out some Sunday, and I said that I would ask Uncle William and Uncle Henry and Cousin Ferdinand and Cousin Willie and if they all consented to come I would go. I hope it was not a forward thing to do.

I forgot when I was talking of work to say that Uncle Henry got work the very second day that we were here. He works down at the docks where the ships are. I think he supervises the incoming and outgoing of the American navy. It is called being a stevedore, and no doubt his being an Admiral helped him to get it. He hopes to get a certificate presently to be a Barge Master, which will put him in charge of the canals. But there is a very difficult examination to go through and Uncle Henry is working for it at night out of a book. He has to take up Vulgar Fractions which, of course, none of our High Seas Command were asked to learn. But Uncle Henry is stooping to them.

So now, I think, everything will go well.

CHAPTER IV

Uncle's art has failed. It was only yesterday that I was writing in my memoirs of how cheerful and glad I felt to think that Uncle William was going to be able to make his living by art, and now everything is changed again. All the time that Uncle was out on his visit to the picture dealers, I was making plans and thinking what we would do with the money when it came in, so it is very disappointing to have it all come to nothing. I don't know just what happened because Uncle William never gives any details of things. His mind moves too rapidly for that. But he came home with his pictures still under his arm in a perfect fury and raged up and down his room, using very dreadful language.

But after a little while when he grew calmer he explained to me that the Americans are merely swineheads and that art, especially art such as his, is wasted on them. Uncle says that he has no wish to speak harshly of the Americans, but they are pig-dogs. He bears them no ill-will, he says, for what they have done and his heart is free of any spirit of vengeance, but he wishes he had his heel on their necks for about half a minute. He said this with such a strange dreadful snarl that for the moment his face seemed quite changed. But presently when he recovered himself he got quite cheerful again, and said that it was perhaps unseemly in him, as the guest of the American people, to say anything against them. It is strange how Uncle always refers to himself as the guest of the American people. Living in this poor place, in these cheap surroundings, it seems so odd. Often at our meals in the noisy dining-room down in the basement, in the speeches that he makes to the boarders, he talks of himself as the guest of America and he says, "What does America ask in return? Nothing." I can see that Mrs. O'Halloran, the landlady, doesn't like this, because we have not paid her anything for quite a long time, and she has spoken to me about it in the corridor several times.

But when Uncle William makes speeches in the dining-room I think the whole room becomes transformed for him into the banquet room of a palace, and the cheap bracket lamps against the wall turn into a blaze of light and the boarders are all courtiers, and he becomes more and more grandiloquent. He waves his hand towards Uncle Henry and refers to him as "my brother the Admiral," and to me as "the Princess at my side." Some of the people, the meaner ones, begin to laugh and to whisper, and others look uncomfortable and sorry. And it is always on these occasions that Uncle William refers to himself as America's guest, and refers to the Americans as the hospitable nation who have taken him to their heart. I think that when Uncle says this he really believes it; Uncle can believe practically anything if he says it himself.

So, as I say, when he came home yesterday, after failing to sell his pictures, he was at first furious and then he fell into his other mood and he said that, as the guest of a great people, he had found out at last the return he could make to them. He said that he would organise a School of Art, and as soon as he had got the idea he was carried away with it at once and seized a pencil and paper and began making plans for the school and drawing up a list of the instructors needed. He asked first who could be Principal, or President, of the School, and decided that he would have to be that himself as he knew of no one but himself who had the peculiar power of organisation needed for it. All the technical instructors, he said, must be absolutely the best, each one a master in his own line. So he wrote down at the top of his list, Instructor in Oils, and reflected a little, with his head in his hand, as to who could do that. Presently he sighed and said that as far as he knew there was no one; he'd have to do that himself. Then he wrote down Instructor in Water Colour, and as soon as he had written it he said right off that he would have to take that over too; there was no one else that he could trust it to. Then he said, "Now, let me see, Perspective, Freehand, and Crayon Work. I need three men: three men of the first class. Can I get them? I doubt it. Let me think what can be done."

He walked up and down the room a little with his hands behind his back and his head sunk in thought while he murmured, "Three men? Three men? But Ha! why THREE? Why not, if sufficiently gifted, ONE man?"

But just when he was saying this there was a knock at the door and Mrs. O'Halloran came in. I knew at once what she had come for, because she had been threatening to do it, and so I felt dreadfully nervous when she began to say that our bill at the house had gone unpaid too long and that we must pay her at once what we owed her. It took some time before Uncle William understood what she was talking about, but when he did he became dreadfully frigid and polite. He said, "Let me understand clearly, madame, just what it is that you wish to say: do I apprehend that you are saying that my account here for our maintenance is now due and payable?" Mrs. O'Halloran said yes, she was. And Uncle said, "Let me endeavour to grasp your meaning exactly: am I correct in thinking that you mean I owe you money?" Mrs. O'Halloran said that was what she meant. Uncle said, "Let me try to apprehend just as accurately as possible what it is that you are trying to tell me: is my surmise correct that you are implying that it is time that I settled up my bill?"

Mrs. O'Halloran said, "Yes," but I could see that by this time she was getting quite flustered because there was something so dreadfully chilling in Uncle's manner: his tone in a way was courtesy itself, but there was something in it calculated to make Mrs. O'Halloran feel that she had committed a dreadful breach in what she had done. Uncle William told me afterwards that to mention money to a prince is not a permissible thing, and that no true Hohenzollern has ever allowed the word "bill" to be said in his presence, and that for this reason he had tried, out of courtesy, to give the woman every chance to withdraw her words and had only administered a reprimand to her when she failed to do so. Certainly it was a dreadful rebuke that he gave her. He told her that he must insist on this topic being dismissed and never raised again: that he could allow no such discussion: the subject was one, he said, that he must absolutely refuse to entertain: he did not wish, he said, to speak with undue severity, but he had better make it plain that if there were any renewal of this discussion he should feel it impossible to remain in the house.

While Uncle William was saying all this Mrs. O'Halloran was getting more and more confused and angry, and when Uncle finally opened the door for her with cold dignity, she backed out of it and found herself outside the room without seeming to know what she was doing. Presently I could hear her down in the scullery below, rattling dishes and saying that she was just as good as anybody.

But Uncle William seemed to be wonderfully calmed and elevated after this scene, and said, "Princess, bring me my flute." I brought it to him and he sat by the window and leaned his head out over the back lane and played our dear old German melodies, till somebody threw a boot at him. The people about here are not musical. But meantime Uncle William had forgotten all about the School of Art, and he said no more about it.

Next Day

To-day a dreadful thing has happened. The police have come into the house and have taken Cousin Willie away. He is now in a place called The Tombs, and Mr. Peters says that he will be sent to the great prison at Sing-Sing. He is to be tried for robbery and for stabbing with intent to kill.

It was very dreadful when they came to take him. I was so glad that Uncle William was not here to see it all. But it was in the morning and he had gone out to see a steamship company about being president of it, and I was tidying up our rooms, because Mrs. O'Halloran won't tidy them up any more or let the coloured servant tidy them up until we pay her more money. She said that to me, but I think she is afraid to say it to Uncle William. So I mean to do the work now while Uncle is out and not let him know.

This morning, in the middle of the morning, while I was working, all of a sudden I heard the street door open and slam and some one rushing up the stairway: and then Cousin Willie broke into the room, all panting and excited, and his face grey with fright and gasping out, "Hide me, hide me!" He ran from room to room whining and hysterical, and his breath coming in a sort of sob, but he seemed incapable of deciding what to do. I would have hidden him if I could, but at the very next moment I heard the policemen coming in below, and the voice of the landlady. Then they came upstairs, big strong-looking men in blue, any one of whom could have choked Cousin Willie with one hand. Cousin Willie ran to and fro like a cornered rat, and two of the men seized him and then I think he must have been beside himself with fear for I saw his teeth bite into the man's hand that held him, and one of the policemen struck him hard with his wooden club across the head and he fell limp to the floor. They dragged him down the stairway like that and I followed them down, but there was nothing that I could do. I saw them lift Cousin Willie into a closed black wagon that stood at the street door with quite a little crowd of people gathered about it already, all excited and leering as if it were a show. And then they drove away with him and I came in and went upstairs and sat down in Uncle's room but I could not work any more. A little later on Mr. Peters came to the house,--I don't know why, because it was not for the ice as he had his other clothes on,--and he came upstairs and sat down and told me about what had happened. It seemed a strange thing to receive him upstairs in Uncle's bedroom like that, but I was so upset that I did not think about it at the time. Mr. Peters had been on our street with his ice wagon when the police came, though I did not see him. But he saw me, he said, standing at the door. And I think he must have gone home and changed his things and come back again, but I did not ask him.

He told me that Cousin Willie had stabbed a man, or at least a boy, that was in charge of a jewelry shop, and that the boy might die. Cousin Willie, Mr. Peters says, has been stealing jewelry nearly ever since we came here and the police have been watching him but he did not know this and so he had grown quite foolhardy, and this morning in broad daylight he went into some sort of jewelry or pawn shop where there was only a boy watching the shop, and the boy was a cripple. Cousin Willie had planned to hide the things under his coat and to sneak out but the boy saw what he was doing and cried out, and when Cousin Willie tried to break out of the shop he hobbled to the door and threw himself in the way. And then it was that Cousin Willie stabbed him with his sheath-knife,--the one that I had seen in his room,--and ran. But already there was a great outcry and the people followed on his tracks and shouted to the police, and so they easily ran him down.

All of this Mr. Peters told me, but he couldn't stay very long and had to go again. He says he is going to see what can be done for Cousin Willie but I am afraid that he doesn't feel very sorry for him; but after Mr. Peters had gone I could not help going on thinking about it all and it seemed to me as if Cousin Willie had not altogether had a fair chance in life. Common people are brought up in fear of prison and punishment and they learn to do what they should. But Cousin Willie was brought up as a prince and was above imprisonment and things like that. And in any case he seemed, when the big men seized hold of him, such a paltry and miserable thing.

Later on in the day Uncle William came home and I had to tell him all about Cousin Willie. I had feared that he would be dreadfully upset, but he was much less disturbed than I had thought. Indeed it is quite wonderful the way in which Uncle can detach his mind from things.

I told him that Mr. Peters had said that Cousin Willie must go to Sing-Sing, and Uncle said, "Ha! a fortress?" So I told him that I thought it was. After that he asked if Cousin Willie was in his uniform at the time, and when I said that he was not, Uncle said "That may make it more difficult." Of course Cousin Willie has no uniform here in America and doesn't wear any, but I notice that Uncle William begins to mix up our old life with our life here and seems sometimes quite confused and wandering; at least other people would think him so. He went on talking quite a long time about what had happened and he said that there is an almost exact precedent for the "incident" (that's what he calls it) in the Zabern Case. I don't remember much about that, as it was years ago, before the war, but Uncle William said that it was a similar case of an officer finding himself compelled to pass his sword once through a cripple (only once, Uncle says) in order to clear himself a way on the sidewalk. Uncle quoted a good many other precedents for passing swords through civilians, but he says that this is the best one.

In the evening Cousin Ferdinand and Uncle Henry came over. Uncle Henry seemed very gloomy and depressed about what had happened and said very little, but Cousin Ferdinand was very much excited and angry. He said what is the good of all his honesty and his industry if he is to be disgraced like this: he asked of what use is his uprightness and business integrity if he is to have a first cousin in Sing-Sing. He said that if it was known that he had a cousin there it would damage him with his best trade to an incalculable extent. But later on he quieted down and said that perhaps with a certain part of his trade it would work the other way. Uncle Ferdinand has grown to be much interested in what is called here "advertising,"--a thing that he says all kings ought to study--and he decided, after he had got over his first indignation, that Cousin Willie being in Sing-Sing would be a very good advertisement for him. It might bring him, he said, quite a lot of new business; especially if it was known that he refused to help Cousin Willie in any way or to have anything more to do with any of the rest of us, and not to give us any money. He said that this was a point of view which people could respect and admire.

So before he went home he said that we must not expect to see or hear from him any more, unless, of course, things should in some way brighten up, in which case he would come back.

CHAPTER V

It is a long time--nearly three months--since I have added anything to my memoirs. The truth is I find it very hard to write memoirs here. For one thing nobody else seems to do it. Mrs. O'Halloran tells me that she never thinks of writing memoirs at all. At the Potsdam palace it was different. We all wrote memoirs. Eugenia of Pless did, and Cecilia did, and I did, and all of us. We all had our memoir books with little silver padlocks and keys. We were brought up to do it because it helped us to realise how important everything was that we did and how important all the people about us were. It was wonderful to realise that in the old life one met every day great world figures like Prince Rasselwitz-Windischkopf, the Grand Falconer of Reuss, and the Grand Duke of Schlitzin-Mein, and Field Marshall Topoff, General-in-Chief of the army of Schwarzburg-Rudolstadt. There are no such figures as these in America.

But another reason for not writing has been that things have been going so badly with us. Uncle William still has no work and he seems to be getting older and more broken and stranger in his talk every day. He is very shabby now in spite of all I can do with my needle, but he becomes more grandiloquent and consequential all the time. Some of the mean looking young men at this boarding house have christened him "The Emperor"--which seems a strange thing for them to have picked upon, and they draw him out in his talk, and when they meet him they make mock salutes to him which Uncle returns with very great dignity. Quite a lot of the people on the nearby streets have taken it up and when they see Uncle come along they make him military salutes. Uncle gets quite pleased and flushed as he goes along the street and answers the salutes with a sort of military bow.

He is quite happy when he is out of doors explaining to me with his stick the plans he has for rebuilding New York and turning the Hudson River to make it run the other way. But when he comes in he falls into the most dreadful depression and sometimes at night I hear him walking up and down in his room far into the night. Two or three times he has had the same dreadful kind of seizures that he had on board the ship when we came over, and this is always when there is a great wind blowing from the ocean and a storm raging out at sea.

Of course as Uncle has not any work or any position, we are getting poorer and poorer. Cousin Willie has been sent to the fortress at Sing-Sing and Cousin Ferdinand of Bulgaria refuses to know us any more, though, from what we hear, he is getting on wonderfully well in the clothing business and is very soon to open a big new store of which he is to be the general manager. Cousin Karl is now the Third Assistant Head-Waiter at the King George Hotel, and in the sphere in which he moves it is impossible for him to acknowledge any relationship with us. I don't know what we should do but that Uncle Henry manages to give us enough of his wages to pay for our board and lodging. Uncle Henry has passed his Naval Examination and is now appointed to a quite high command. It is called a Barge Master. They refused to accept his certificate of a German Admiral, so he had to study very hard, but at last he got his qualification and is now in charge of long voyages on the canals.

I am very glad that Uncle Henry's command turned out to be on canals instead of on the high seas, as it makes it so much more German. Of course Uncle Henry had splendid experience in the Kiel Canal all through the four years of the war, and it is bound to come in. So he goes away now on quite long voyages, often of two or three weeks at a time, and for all this time he is in chief charge of his barge and has to work out all the navigation. Sometimes Uncle Henry takes bricks and sometimes sand. He says it is a great responsibility to feel oneself answerable for the safety of a whole barge-full of bricks or sand. It is quite different from what he did in the German navy, because there it was only a question of the sailors and for most of the time, as I have heard Uncle William and Uncle Henry say, we had plenty of them, but here with bricks and sand it is different. Uncle Henry says that if his barge was wrecked he would lose his job. This makes it a very different thing from being a royal admiral.

But Uncle William all through the last three months has failed first at one thing and then at another. After all his plans for selling pictures had come to nothing he decided, very reluctantly that he would go into business. He only reached this decision after a great deal of anxious thought because, of course, business is a degradation. It involves taking money for doing things and this, Uncle William says, no prince can consent to do. But at last, after deep thought, Uncle said, "The die is cast," and sat down and wrote a letter offering to take over the presidency of the United States Steel Corporation. We spent two or three anxious days waiting for the answer. Uncle was very firm and kept repeating, "I have set my hand to it, and I will do it," but I was certain that he was sorry about it and it was a great relief when the answer came at last--it took days and days, evidently, for them to decide about it--in which the corporation said that they would "worry along" as they were. Uncle explained to me what "worrying along" meant and he said that he admired their spirit. But that ended all talk of his going into business and I am sure that we were both glad.

After that Uncle William decided that it was necessary for me to marry in a way to restore our fortunes and he decided to offer me to a State Governor. He asked me if I had any choice of States, and I said no. Of course I should not have wished to marry a state governor, but I knew my duty towards Uncle William and I said nothing. So Uncle got a map of the United States and he decided to marry me to the Governor of Texas. He told me that I could have two weeks to arrange my supply of household linen and my trousseau to take to Texas, and he wrote at once to the Governor. He showed me what he wrote and it was a very formal letter. I think that Uncle's mind gets more and more confused as to where he is and what he is and he wrote in quite the old strain and I noticed that he signed himself, "Your brother, William." Perhaps it was on that account that we had no answer to the letter. Uncle seemed to forget all about it very soon and I was glad that it was so, and that I had escaped going to the court of Texas.

All this time Mr. Peters has been very kind. He comes to the house with his ice every day and sometimes when Uncle Henry is here he comes in with him and smokes in the evenings. One day he brought a beautiful bunch of chrysanthemums for Uncle William, and another day a lovely nosegay of violets for Uncle Henry. And one Sunday he took us out for a beautiful drive with one of his ice-horses in a carriage called a buggy, with three seats. Uncle William sat with Mr. Peters in the front seat, and Uncle Henry and Cousin Ferdinand (it was the last time he came to see us) sat behind them and there was a little seat at the back in which I sat. It was a lovely drive and Uncle William pointed out to Mr. Peters all the things of interest, and Cousin Ferdinand smoked big cigars and told Uncle Henry all about the clothing trade, and I listened to them all and enjoyed it very much indeed. But I was afraid afterwards that it was a very bold and unconventional thing to do, and perhaps Mr. Peters felt that he had asked too much because he did not invite me to drive again.

But he is always very kind and thoughtful.

One Sunday afternoon he came to see us, thinking by mistake that Uncle William and Uncle Henry were there, but they weren't, and his manner seemed so strange and constrained that I was certain that there was something that he was trying to say and it made me dreadfully nervous and confused. And at last quite suddenly he said that there was something that he wanted to ask me if I wouldn't think it a liberty. My breath stopped and I couldn't speak, and then he went on to ask if he might lend us twenty-five dollars. He got very red in the face when he said it and he began counting out the money on the sofa, and somehow I hadn't expected that it was money and began to cry. But I told Mr. Peters that of course we couldn't think of taking any money, and I begged him to pick it up again and then I began to try to tell him about how hard it was to get along and to ask him to get work for Uncle William, but I started to cry again. Mr. Peters came over to my chair and took hold of the arm of it and told me not to cry. Somehow his touch on the arm of the chair thrilled all through me and though I knew that it was wrong I let him keep it there and even let him stroke the upholstery and I don't know just what would have happened but at that very minute Uncle William came in. He was most courteous to Mr. Peters and expressed his apologies for having been out and said that it must have been extremely depressing for Mr. Peters to find that he was not at home, and he thanked him for putting himself to the inconvenience of waiting. And a little while after that Mr. Peters left.

The Next Day

Mr. Peters came back this morning and said that he had got work for Uncle William. So I was delighted. He said that Uncle will make a first class "street man," and that he has arranged for a line of goods for him and that he has a "territory" that Uncle can occupy. He showed me a flat cardboard box filled with lead pencils and shoe-strings and little badges and buttons with inscriptions on them, and he says these are what is called a "line," and that Uncle can take out this line and do splendidly. I don't quite understand yet who makes the appointment to be a street man or what influence it takes or what it means to have a territory, but Mr. Peters explained that there is a man who is retiring from being a street man and that Uncle can take his place and can have both sides of the Bowery, which sounds very pretty indeed.

At first I didn't understand--because Mr. Peters hesitated a good deal in telling me about it--that if Uncle gets this appointment, it will mean that he will sell things in the street. But as soon as I understood this I felt that Uncle William would scorn to do anything like this, as the degradation would be the same as being President of the Steel Corporation. So I was much surprised to find that when Uncle came in he didn't look at it that way at all. He looked at the box of badges and buttons and things, and he said at once, "Ha! Orders of Distinction! An excellent idea." He picked up a silly little white button with the motto "Welcome to New York," and he said "Admirable! That shall be the first class." And there was a little lead spoon with "Souvenir of the Bowery" that he made the second class. He started arranging and rearranging all the things in the box, just as he used to arrange the orders and decorations at the Palace. Only those were REAL things such as the Order of the Red Feather, and The Insignia of the Black Duck, and these were only poor tin baubles. But I could see that Uncle no longer knows the difference, and as his fingers fumbled among these silly things he was quite trembling and eager to begin, like a child waiting for to-morrow.

CHAPTER VI

It is a year or nearly a year since I wrote in my memoirs, and I only add to them now because things have happened which mean that I shall never write any more.

Mr. Peters and I were married last autumn. He asked me if I would marry him the day that he held the arm of my chair in the boarding house where we used to live. At first I never thought that Uncle William would permit it, because of the hopeless difference of birth. But it turned out that there was no difficulty at all. Uncle's mind was always so wonderful that he could find a way out of anything provided that he wanted to. So he conferred on Mr. Peters an Order that raised him right up in birth so that he came level with me. Uncle said that he could have lifted him higher still if need be but that as I was only, in our old life, of a younger branch of the family, it was not necessary to lift Mr. Peters to the very top. He takes precedence, Uncle said, just below Uncle Henry of Prussia and just above an Archbishop.

It is so pleasant to think--now that poor Uncle William is gone--that my marriage was with his full consent.

But even after Uncle William had given his formal consent, I didn't want to get married till I could leave him safely. Only he got along so well in his "territory" of the Bowery from the very start that he was soon quite all right. He used to go out every morning with his trayful of badges and pencils and shoe-strings and he was a success at once. All the people got to know him by sight and they would say when they saw him, "Here comes the Emperor," or "Here comes Old Dutch," and very often there would be quite a little crowd round him buying his things. Uncle regarded himself always as conferring a great dignity on any one that he sold a badge to, but he was very capricious and he had certain buttons and badges that he would only part with as a very special favour and honour. Uncle got on so fast that presently Cousin Ferdinand decided that it would be all right to know him again and so he came over and made a reconciliation and took away Uncle's money,--it was all in small coins,--in a bag to invest for him.

So when everything was all right with Uncle William, Mr. Peters and I were married and it was on our wedding morning that Uncle conferred the Order on my husband which made me very proud. That was a year ago, and since then we have lived in a very fine place of our own with four rooms, all to ourselves, and a gallery at the back. I have cooked all the meals and done all the work of our apartment, except just at the time when our little boy was born. We both think he is a very wonderful child. At first I wanted to call him after the Hohenzollerns and to name him William Frederick Charles Mary Augustus Francis Felix, but somehow it seemed out of place and so we have called him simply Joe Peters. I think it sounds better. Uncle William drew up an act of abnegation of Joe, whereby he gives up all claim to a reversion of the throne of Prussia, Brunswick and Waldeck. I was sorry for this at first but Uncle said that all the Hohenzollerns had done it and had made just as great a sacrifice as Joe has in doing it. But my husband says that under the constitution of the United States, Joe can be President, which I think I will like better.

It was one day last week that Uncle William met with the accident that caused his death. He had walked far away from his "territory" up to where the Great Park is, because in this lovely spring weather he liked to wander about. And he came to where there was a great crowd of people gathered to see the unveiling of a new monument. It is called the Lusitania Monument and it is put up in memory of the people that were lost when one of our war boats fought the English cruiser Lusitania. There were a lot of soldiers lining the streets and regiments of cavalry riding between. And it seems that when Uncle William saw the crowd and the soldiers he was drawn nearer and nearer by a sort of curiosity, and when he saw the great white veil drawn away from the monument, and read the word "Lusitania" that is carved in large letters across the base, he screamed out in a sudden fear, and clashed among the horses of the cavalry and was ridden down.

They carried him to the hospital, but he never spoke again, and died on the next day but one. My husband would not let me go to see him, as he was not conscious and it could do no good, but after Uncle William was dead they let me see him in his coffin.

Lying there he seemed such a pitiful and ghastly lump of clay that it seemed strange that he could, in his old life, have vexed the world as he did.

I had thought that when Uncle William died there would have been long accounts of him in the papers; at least I couldn't help thinking so, by a sort of confusion of mind, as it is hard to get used to things as they are and to remember that our other life is unknown here and that we are known only as ourselves.

But though I looked in all the papers I could find nothing except one little notice, which I cut out of an evening paper and which I put in here as a conclusion to my memoirs.

THE "EMPEROR" DEAD

Unique Character of the East Side Passes Away

A unique and interesting character, a familiar figure
of the East Side of the City, has been lost from our
streets with the death of William Hohen lost Thursday

in the Pauper Hospital, to which he had been brought as the result of injuries sustained in a street accident at the Lusitania celebration. Hohen, who was about sixty-five years of age, was an immigrant out of Germany after the troubles of the Great War. He had been for a year or more a street pedler on the Bowery, where he sold souvenir buttons and various little trinkets. The old man appears to have been the victim of a harmless hallucination whereby he thought himself a person of Royal distinction and in his fancy converted the box of wares that he carried into Orders of Chivalry and decorations of Knighthood. The effect of this strange fancy was heightened by an attempt at military bearing which, comic though it was in so old and ragged a figure, was not without a touch of pathos. Some fancied resemblance to the former Kaiser had earned for Hohen the designation of the "Emperor," of which he appeared inordinately proud. But those who knew Hohen by sight assure us that the resemblance to the former ruler of Germany, who with all his faults made a splendid and imposing appearance, was of a purely superficial character. It would, alas! have been well for the world if the lot of William Hohenzollern had fallen on the lines of the simple and pathetic "Emperor" of the Bowery.

II.--With the Bolsheviks in Berlin

Two years ago as my readers will remember,--but of course they don't,--I made a secret visit to Germany during the height of the war. It was obviously quite impossible at that time to disclose the means whereby I made my way across the frontier. I therefore adopted the familiar literary device of professing to have been transported to Germany in a dream. In that state I was supposed to be conducted about the country by my friend Count Boob von Boobenstein, whom I had known years before as a waiter in Toronto, to see GERMANY FROM WITHIN, and to report upon it in the Allied press.

What I wrote attracted some attention. So the German Government--feeling, perhaps, that the prestige of their own spy system was at stake--published a white paper, --or a green paper,--I forget which,--in denial of all my adventures and disclosures. In this they proved (1) that all entry into Germany by dreams had been expressly forbidden of the High General Command; (2) that astral bodies were prohibited and (3) that nobody else but the Kaiser was allowed to have visions. They claimed therefore (1) that my article was a fabrication and (2) that for all they knew it was humorous. There the matter ended until it can be taken up at the General Peace Table.

But as soon as I heard that the People's Revolution had taken place in Berlin I determined to make a second visit.

This time I had no difficulty about the frontier whatever. I simply put on the costume of a British admiral and walked in.

"Three Cheers for the British Navy!" said the first official whom I met. He threw his hat in the air and the peasants standing about raised a cheer. It was my first view of the marvellous adaptability of this great people. I noticed that many of them were wearing little buttons with pictures of Jellicoe and Beatty.

At my own request I was conducted at once to the nearest railway station.

"So your Excellency wishes to go to Berlin?" said the stationmaster.

"Yes," I replied, "I want to see something of the people's revolution."

The stationmaster looked at his watch.

"That Revolution is over," he said.

"Too bad!" I exclaimed.

"Not at all. A much better one is in progress, quite the best Revolution that we have had. It is called--Johann, hand me that proclamation of yesterday--the Workmen and Soldiers Revolution."

"What's it about?" I asked.

"The basis of it," said the stationmaster, "or what we Germans call the Fundamental Ground Foundation, is universal love. They hanged all the leaders of the Old Revolution yesterday."

"When can I get a train?" I inquired.

"Your Excellency shall have a special train at once, Sir," he continued with a sudden burst of feeling, while a tear swelled in his eye. "The sight of your uniform calls forth all our gratitude. My three sons enlisted in our German Navy. For four years they have been at Kiel, comfortably fed, playing dominos. They are now at home all safe and happy. Had your brave navy relaxed its vigilance for a moment those boys might have had to go out on the sea, a thing they had never done. Please God," concluded the good old man, removing his hat a moment, "no German sailor now will ever have to go to sea."

I pass over my journey to Berlin. Interesting and varied as were the scenes through which I passed they gave me but little light upon the true situation of the country: indeed I may say without exaggeration that they gave me as little--or even more so--as the press reports of our talented newspaper correspondents. The food situation seemed particularly perplexing. A well-to-do merchant from Bremen who travelled for some distance in my train assured me that there was plenty of food in Germany, except of course for the poor. Distress, he said, was confined entirely to these. Similarly a Prussian gentleman who looked very like a soldier, but who assured me with some heat that he was a commercial traveller, told me the same thing: There were no cases of starvation, he said, except among the very poor.

The aspect of the people too, at the stations and in the towns we passed, puzzled me. There were no uniforms, no soldiers. But I was amazed at the number of commercial travellers, Lutheran ministers, photographers, and so forth, and the odd resemblance they presented, in spite of their innocent costumes, to the arrogant and ubiquitous military officers whom I had observed on my former visit.

But I was too anxious to reach Berlin to pay much attention to the details of my journey.

Even when I at last reached the capital, I arrived as I had feared, too late.

"Your Excellency," said a courteous official at the railway station, to whom my naval uniform acted as a sufficient passport. "The Revolution of which you speak is over. Its leaders were arrested yesterday. But you shall not be disappointed. There is a better one. It is called the Comrades' Revolution of the Bolsheviks. The chief Executive was installed yesterday."

"Would it be possible for me to see him?" I asked.

"Nothing simpler, Excellency," he continued as a tear rose in his eye. "My four sons,--"

"I know," I said; "your four sons are in the German Navy. It is enough. Can you take me to the Leader?"

"I can and will," said the official. "He is sitting now in the Free Palace of all the German People, once usurped by the Hohenzollern Tyrant. The doors are guarded by machine guns. But I can take you direct from here through a back way. Come."

We passed out from the station, across a street and through a maze of little stairways, and passages into the heart of the great building that had been the offices of the Imperial Government.

"Enter this room. Do not knock," said my guide. "Good bye."

In another moment I found myself face to face with the chief comrade of the Bolsheviks.

He gave a sudden start as he looked at me, but instantly collected himself.

He was sitting with his big boots up on the mahogany desk, a cigar at an edge-ways angle in his mouth. His hair under his sheepskin cap was shaggy, and his beard stubbly and unshaven. His dress was slovenly and there was a big knife in his belt. A revolver lay on the desk beside him. I had never seen a Bolshevik before but I knew at sight that he must be one.

"You say you were here in Berlin once before?" he questioned, and he added before I had time to answer: "When you speak don't call me 'Excellency' or 'Sereneness' or anything of that sort; just call me 'brother' or 'comrade.' This is the era of freedom. You're as good as I am, or nearly."

"Thank you," I said.

"Don't be so damn polite," he snarled. "No good comrade ever says 'thank you.' So you were here in Berlin before?"

"Yes," I answered, "I was here writing up Germany from Within in the middle of the war."

"The war, the war!" he murmured, in a sort of wail or whine. "Take notice, comrade, that I weep when I speak of it. If you write anything about me be sure to say that I cried when the war was mentioned. We Germans have been so misjudged. When I think of the devastation of France and Belgium I weep."

He drew a greasy, red handkerchief from his pocket and began to sob. "To think of the loss of all those English merchant ships!"

"Oh, you needn't worry," I said, "it's all going to be paid for."

"Oh I hope so, I do hope so," said the Bolshevik chief. "What a regret it is to us Germans to think that unfortunately we are not able to help pay for it; but you English--you are so generous--how much we have admired your noble hearts--so kind, so generous to the vanquished..."

His voice had subsided into a sort of whine.

But at this moment there was a loud knocking at the door. The Bolshevik hastily wiped the tears from his face and put away his handkerchief.

"How do I look?" he asked anxiously. "Not humane, I hope? Not soft?"

"Oh, no," I said, "quite tough."

"That's good," he answered. "That's good. But am I tough ENOUGH?"

He hastily shoved his hands through his hair.

"Quick," he said, "hand me that piece of chewing tobacco. Now then. Come in!"

The door swung open.

A man in a costume much like the leader's swaggered into the room. He had a bundle of papers in his hands, and seemed to be some sort of military secretary.

"Ha! comrade!" he said, with easy familiarity. "Here are the death warrants!"

"Death warrants!" said the Bolshevik. "Of the leaders of the late Revolution?

Excellent! And a good bundle of them! One moment while I sign them."

He began rapidly signing the warrants, one after the other.

"Comrade," said the secretary in a surly tone, "you are not chewing tobacco!"

"Yes I am, yes I am," said the leader, "or, at least, I was just going to."

He bit a huge piece out of his plug, with what seemed to me an evident distaste, and began to chew furiously.

"It is well," said the other. "Remember comrade, that you are watched. It was reported last night to the Executive Committee of the Circle of the Brothers that you chewed no tobacco all day yesterday. Be warned, comrade. This is a free and independent republic. We will stand for no aristocratic nonsense. But whom have you here?" he added, breaking off in his speech, as if he noticed me for the first time. "What dog is this?"

"Hush," said the leader, "he is a representative of the foreign press, a newspaper reporter."

"Your pardon," said the secretary. "I took you by your dress for a prince. A representative of the great and enlightened press of the Allies, I presume. How deeply we admire in Germany the press of England! Let me kiss you."

"Oh, don't trouble," I said, "it's not worth while."

"Say, at least, when you write to your paper, that I offered to kiss you, will you not?"

Meantime, the leader had finished signing the papers. The secretary took them and swung on his heels with something between a military bow and a drunken swagger. "Remember, comrade," he said in a threatening tone as he passed out, "you are watched."

The Bolshevik leader looked after him with something of a shudder.

"Excuse me a moment," he said, "while I go and get rid of this tobacco."

He got up from his chair and walked away towards the door of an inner room. As he did so, there struck me something strangely familiar in his gait and figure. Conceal it as he might, there was still the stiff wooden movement of a Prussian general beneath his assumed swagger. The poise of his head still seemed to suggest the pointed helmet of the Prussian. I could without effort imagine a military cloak about his shoulders instead of his Bolshevik sheepskin.

Then, all in a moment, as he re-entered the room, I recalled exactly who he was.

"My friend," I said, reaching out my hand, "pardon me for not knowing you at once. I recognize you now..."

"Hush," said the Bolshevik. "Don't speak! I never saw you in my life."

"Nonsense," I said, "I knew you years ago in Canada when you were disguised as a waiter. And you it was who conducted me through Germany two years ago when I made my war visit. You are no more a Bolshevik than I am. You are General Count Boob von Boobenstein."

The general sank down in his chair, his face pale beneath its plaster of rouge.

"Hush!" he said. "If they learn it, it is death."

"My dear Boob," I said, "not a word shall pass my lips."

The general grasped my hand. "The true spirit," he said, "the true English comradeship; how deeply we admire it in Germany!"

"I am sure you do," I answered. "But tell me, what is the meaning of all this? Why are you a Bolshevik?"

"We all are," said the count, dropping his assumed rough voice, and speaking in a tone of quiet melancholy. "It's the only thing to be. But come," he added, getting up from his chair, "I took you once through Berlin in war time. Let me take you out again and show you Berlin under the Bolsheviks."

"I shall be only too happy," I said.

"I shall leave my pistols and knives here," said Boobenstein, "and if you will excuse me I shall change my costume a little. To appear as I am would excite too much enthusiasm. I shall walk out with you in the simple costume of a gentleman. It's a risky thing to do in Berlin, but I'll chance it."

The count retired, and presently returned dressed in the quiet bell-shaped purple coat, the simple scarlet tie, the pea-green hat and the white spats that mark the German gentleman all the world over.

"Bless me, Count," I said, "you look just like Bernstorff."

"Hush," said the count. "Don't mention him. He's here in Berlin."

"What's he doing?" I asked.

"He's a Bolshevik; one of our leaders; he's just been elected president of the Scavengers Union. They say he's the very man for it. But come along, and, by the way, when we get into the street talk English and only English. There's getting to be a prejudice here against German."

We passed out of the door and through the spacious corridors and down the stairways of the great building. All about were little groups of ferocious looking men, dressed like stage Russians, all chewing tobacco and redolent of alcohol.

"Who are all these people?" I said to the count in a low voice.

"Bolsheviks," he whispered. "At least they aren't really. You see that group in the corner?

"The ones with the long knives," I said.

"Yes. They are, or at least they were, the orchestra of the Berlin Opera. They are now the Bolshevik Music Commission. They are here this morning to see about getting their second violinist hanged."

"Why not the first?" I asked.

"They had him hanged yesterday. Both cases are quite clear. The men undoubtedly favoured the war: one, at least, of them openly spoke in disparagement of President Wilson. But come along. Let me show you our new city."

We stepped out upon the great square which faced the building. How completely it was changed from the Berlin that I had known! My attention was at once arrested by the new and glaring signboards at the shops and hotels, and the streamers with mottos suspended across the streets. I realised as I read them the marvellous adaptability of the German people and their magnanimity towards their enemies. Conspicuous in huge lettering was HOTEL PRESIDENT WILSON, and close beside it CABARET QUEEN MARY: ENGLISH DANCING. The square itself, which I remembered as the Kaiserplatz, was now renamed on huge signboards GRAND SQUARE OF THE BRITISH NAVY. Not far off one noticed the RESTAURANT MARSHAL FOCH, side by side with the ROOSEVELT SALOON and the BEER GARDEN GEORGE V.

But the change in the appearance and costume of the men who crowded the streets was even more notable. The uniforms and the pointed helmets of two years ago had vanished utterly. The men that one saw retained indeed their German stoutness, their flabby faces, and their big spectacles. But they were now dressed for the most part in the costume of the Russian Monjik, while some of them appeared in American wideawakes and Kentucky frock coats, or in English stove-pipe hats and morning coats. A few of the stouter were in Highland costume.

"You are amazed," said Boobenstein as we stood a moment looking at the motley crowd. "What does it mean?" I asked.

"One moment," said the count. "I will first summon a taxi. It will be more convenient to talk as we ride."

He whistled and there presently came lumbering to our side an ancient and decrepit vehicle which would have excited my laughter but for the seriousness of the count's face. The top of the conveyance had evidently long since been torn off leaving, only the frame: the copper fastenings had been removed: the tires were gone: the doors were altogether missing.

"Our new 1919 model," said the count. "Observe the absence of the old-fashioned rubber tires, still used by the less progressive peoples. Our chemists found that riding on rubber was bad for the eye-sight. Note, too, the time saved by not having any doors."

"Admirable," I said.

We seated ourselves in the crazy conveyance, the count whispered to the chauffeur an address which my ear failed to catch and we started off at a lumbering pace along the street.

"And now tell me, Boobenstein," I said, "what does it all mean, the foreign signs and the strange costumes?"

"My dear sir" he replied, "it is merely a further proof of our German adaptability. Having failed to conquer the world by war we now propose to conquer it by the arts of peace: Those people, for example, that you see in Scotch costumes are members of our Highland Mission about to start for Scotland to carry to the Scotch the good news that the war is a thing of the past, that the German people forgive all wrongs and are prepared to offer a line of manufactured goods as per catalogue sample."

"Wonderful," I said.

"Is it not?" said Von Boobenstein. "We call it the From Germany Out movement. It is being organised in great detail by our Step from Under Committee. They claim that already four million German voters are pledged to forget the war and to forgive the Allies. All that we now ask is to be able to put our hands upon the villains who made this war, no matter how humble their station may be, and execute them after a fair trial or possibly before."

The count spoke with great sincerity and earnestness. "But come along," he added. "I want to drive you about the city and show you a few of the leading features of our new national reconstruction. We can talk as we go."

"But Von Boobenstein," I said, "you speak of the people who made the war; surely you were all in favour of it?"

"In favour of it! We were all against it."

"But the Kaiser," I protested.

"The Kaiser, my poor master! How he worked to prevent the war! Day and night; even before anybody else had heard of it. 'Boob,' he said to me one day with tears in his eyes, 'this war must be stopped.' 'Which war, your Serenity,' I asked. 'The war that is coming next month,' he answered, 'I look to you, Count Boobenstein,' he continued, 'to bear witness that I am doing my utmost to stop it a month before the English Government has heard of it.'"

While we were thus speaking our taxi had taken us out of the roar and hubbub of the main thoroughfare into the quiet of a side street. It now drew up at the door of an unpretentious dwelling in the window of which I observed a large printed card with the legend

REVEREND MR. TIBBITS
Private Tuition, English, Navigation,
and other Branches

We entered and were shown by a servant into a little front room where a venerable looking gentleman, evidently a Lutheran minister, was seated in a corner at a writing table. He turned on our entering and at the sight of the uniform which I wore jumped to his feet with a vigorous and unexpected oath.

"It is all right, Admiral," said Count Von Boobenstein. "My friend is not really a sailor."

"Ah!" said the other. "You must excuse me. The sight of that uniform always gives me the jumps."

He came forward to shake hands and as the light fell upon him I recognized the grand old seaman, perhaps the greatest sailor that Germany has ever produced or ever will, Admiral Von Tirpitz.

"My dear Admiral!" I said, warmly. "I thought you were out of the country. Our papers said that you had gone to Switzerland for a rest."

"No," said the Admiral. "I regret to say that I find it impossible to get away."

"Your Allied press," interjected the count, "has greatly maligned our German patriots by reporting that they have left the country. Where better could they trust themselves than in the bosom of their own people? You noticed the cabman of our taxi? He was the former chancellor Von Hertling. You saw that stout woman with the apple cart at the street corner? Frau Bertha Krupp Von Bohlen. All are here, helping to make the new Germany. But come, Admiral, our visitor here is much interested in our plans for the restoration of the Fatherland. I thought that you might care to show him your designs for the new German Navy."

"A new navy!" I exclaimed, while my voice showed the astonishment and admiration that I felt. Here was this gallant old seaman, having just lost an entire navy, setting vigorously to work to make another. "But how can Germany possibly find the money in her present state for the building of new ships?"

"There are not going to be any ships," said the great admiral. "That was our chief mistake in the past in insisting on having ships in the navy. Ships, as the war has shown us, are quite unnecessary to the German plan; they are not part of what I may call the German idea. The new navy will be built inland and elevated on piles and will consist--"

But at this moment a great noise of shouting and sudden tumult could be heard as if from the street.

"Some one is coming," said the admiral hastily. "Reach me my Bible."

"No, no," said the count, seizing me by the arm. "The sound comes from the Great Square. There is trouble. We must hasten back at once."

He dragged me from the house.

We perceived at once, as soon as we came into the main street again, from the excited demeanour of the crowd and from the anxious faces of people running to and fro that something of great moment must be happening.

Everybody was asking of the passer-by, "What is loose? What is it?" Ramshack taxis, similar to the one in which we had driven, forced their way as best they could through the crowded thoroughfare, moving evidently in the direction of the government buildings.

"Hurry, hurry!" said Von Boobenstein, clutching me by the arm, "or we shall be too late. It is as I feared."

"What is it?" I said; "what's the matter?"

"Fool that I was," said the count, "to leave the building. I should have known. And in this costume I am helpless."

We made our way as best we could through the crowd of people, who all seemed moving in the same direction, the count, evidently a prey to the gravest anxiety, talking as if to himself and imprecating his own carelessness.

We turned the corner of a street and reached the edge of the great square. It was filled with a vast concourse of people. At the very moment in which we reached it a great burst of cheering rose from the crowd. We could see over the heads of the people that a man had appeared on the balcony of the Government Building, holding a paper in his hand. His appearance was evidently a signal for the outburst of cheers, accompanied by the waving of handkerchiefs. The man raised his hand in a gesture of authority. German training is deep. Silence fell instantly upon the assembled populace. We had time in the momentary pause to examine, as closely as the distance permitted, the figure upon the balcony. The man was dressed in the blue overall suit of a workingman. He was bare-headed. His features, so far as we could tell, were those of a man well up in years, but his frame was rugged and powerful. Then he began to speak.

"Friends and comrades!" he called out in a great voice that resounded through the square. "I have to announce that a New Revolution has been completed."

A wild cheer woke from the people.

"The Bolsheviks' Republic is overthrown. The Bolsheviks are aristocrats. Let them die."

"Thank Heaven for this costume!" I heard Count Boobenstein murmur at my side. Then he seized his pea-green hat and waved it in the air, shouting: "Down with the Bolsheviks!"

All about us the cry was taken up.

One saw everywhere in the crowd men pulling off their sheepskin coats and tramping them under foot with the shout, "Down with Bolshevism!" To my surprise I observed that most of the men had on blue overalls beneath their Russian costumes. In a few moments the crowd seemed transformed into a vast mass of mechanics.

The speaker raised his hand again. "We have not yet decided what the new Government will be"--

A great cheer from the people.

"Nor do we propose to state who will be the leaders of it."

Renewed cheers.

"But this much we can say. It is to be a free, universal, Pan-German Government of love."

Cheers.

"Meantime, be warned. Whoever speaks against it will be shot: anybody who dares to lift a finger will be hanged. A proclamation of Brotherhood will be posted all over the city. If anybody dares to touch it, or to discuss it, or to look at or to be seen reading it, he will be hanged to a lamp post."

Loud applause greeted this part of the speech while the faces of the people, to my great astonishment, seemed filled with genuine relief and beamed with unmistakable enthusiasm.

"And now," continued the speaker, "I command you, you dogs, to disperse quietly and go home. Move quickly, swine that you are, or we shall open fire upon you with machine guns."

With a last outburst of cheering the crowd broke and dispersed, like a vast theatre audience. On all sides were expressions of joy and satisfaction. "Excellent, wunderschoen!" "He calls us dogs! That's splendid. Swine! Did you hear him say 'Swine'? This is true German Government again at last."

Then just for a moment the burly figure reappeared on the balcony.

"A last word!" he called to the departing crowd. "I omitted to say that all but one of the leaders of the late government are already caught. As soon as we can lay our thumb on the Chief Executive rest assured that he will be hanged."

"Hurrah!" shouted Boobenstein, waving his hat in the air. Then in a whisper to me: "Let us go," he said, "while the going is still good."

We hastened as quickly and unobtrusively as we could through the dispersing multitude, turned into a side street, and on a sign from the count entered a small cabaret or drinking shop, newly named, as its sign showed, THE GLORY OF THE BRITISH COLONIES CAFE.

The count with a deep sigh of relief ordered wine.

"You recognized him, of course?" he said.

"Who?" I asked. "You mean the big working-man that spoke? Who is he?"

"So you didn't recognize him?" said the count. "Well, well, but of course all the rest did. Workingman! It is Field Marshal Hindenburg. It means of course that the same old crowd are back again. That was Ludendorf standing below. I saw it all at once. Perhaps it is the only way. But as for me I shall not go back: I am too deeply compromised: it would be death."

Boobenstein remained for a time in deep thought, his fingers beating a tattoo on the little table. Then he spoke.

"Do you remember," he said, "the old times of long ago when you first knew me?"

"Very well, indeed," I answered. "You were one of the German waiters, or rather, one of the German officers disguised as waiters at McConkey's Restaurant in Toronto."

"I was," said the count. "I carried the beer on a little tray and opened oysters behind a screen. It was a wunderschoen life. Do you think, my good friend, you could get me that job again?"

"Boobenstein," I exclaimed, "I can get you reinstated at once. It will be some small return for your kindness to me in Germany."

"Good," said the count. "Let us sail at once for Canada."

"One thing, however," I said. "You may not know that since you left there are no longer beer waiters in Toronto because there is no beer. All is forbidden."

"Let me understand myself," said the count in astonishment. "No beer!"

"None whatever."

"Wine, then?"

"Absolutely not. All drinking, except of water, is forbidden."

The count rose and stood erect. His figure seemed to regain all its old-time Prussian rigidity. He extended his hand.

"My friend," he said. "I bid you farewell."

"Where are you going to?" I asked.

"My choice is made," said Von Boobenstein. "There are worse things than death. I am about to surrender myself to the German authorities."

III.--Afternoon Tea with the Sultan

A Study of Reconstruction in Turkey

On the very day following the events related in the last chapter, I was surprised and delighted to receive a telegram which read "Come on to Constantinople and write US up too." From the signature I saw that the message was from my old friend Abdul Aziz the Sultan.

I had visited him--as of course my readers will instantly recollect--during the height of the war, and the circumstances of my departure had been such that I should have scarcely ventured to repeat my visit without this express invitation. But on receipt of it, I set out at once by rail for Constantinople.

I was delighted to find that under the new order of things in going from Berlin to Constantinople it was no longer necessary to travel through the barbarous and brutal populations of Germany, Austria and Hungary. The way now runs, though I believe the actual railroad is the same, through the Thuringian Republic, Czecho-Slovakia and Magyaria. It was a source of deep satisfaction to see the scowling and hostile countenances of Germans, Austrians and Hungarians replaced by the cheerful and honest faces of the Thuringians, the Czecho-Slovaks and the Magyarians. Moreover I was assured on all sides that if these faces are not perfectly satisfactory, they will be altered in any way required.

It was very pleasant, too, to find myself once again in the flagstoned halls of the Yildiz Kiosk, the Sultan's palace. My little friend Abdul Aziz rose at once from his cushioned divan under a lemon tree and came shuffling in his big slippers to meet me, a smile of welcome on his face. He seemed, to my surprise, radiant with happiness. The disasters attributed by the allied press to his unhappy country appeared to sit lightly on the little man.

"How is everything going in Turkey?" I asked as we sat down side by side on the cushions.

"Splendid," said Abdul. "I suppose you've heard that we're bankrupt?"

"Bankrupt!" I exclaimed.

"Yes," continued the Sultan, rubbing his hands together with positive enjoyment, "we can't pay a cent: isn't it great? Have some champagne?"

He clapped his hands together and a turbaned attendant appeared with wine on a tray which he served into long-necked glasses.

"I'd rather have tea," I said.

"No, no, don't take tea," he protested. "We've practically cut out afternoon tea here. It's part of our Turkish thrift movement. We're taking champagne instead. Tell me, have you a Thrift Movement like that, where you come from--Canada, I think it is, isn't it?"

"Yes," I answered, "we have one just like that."

"This war finance is glorious stuff, isn't it?" continued the Sultan. "How much do you think we owe?"

"I haven't an idea," I said.

"Wait a minute," said Abdul. He touched a bell and at the sound of it there came shuffling into the room my venerable old acquaintance Toomuch Koffi, the Royal Secretary. But to my surprise he no longer wore his patriarchal beard, his flowing robe and his girdle. He was clean shaven and close cropped and dressed in a short jacket like an American bell boy.

"You remember Toomuch, I think," said Abdul. "I've reconstructed him a little, as you see."

"The Peace of Allah be upon thine head," said Toomuch Koffi to the Sultan, commencing a deep salaam. "What wish sits behind thy forehead that thou shouldst ring the bell for this humble creature of clay to come into the sunlight of thy presence? Tell me, O Lord, if perchance--"

"Here, here," interrupted the Sultan impatiently, "cut all that stuff out, please. That ancient courtesy business won't do, not if this country is to reconstruct itself and come abreast of the great modern democracies. Say to me simply 'What's the trouble?'"

Toomuch bowed, and Abdul continued. "Look in your tablets and see how much our public debt amounts to in American dollars."

The secretary drew forth his tablets and bowed his head a moment in some perplexity over the figures that were scribbled on them. "Multiplication," I heard him murmur, "is an act of the grace of heaven; let me invoke a blessing on FIVE, the perfect number, whereby the Pound Turkish is distributed into the American dollar."

He remained for a few moments with his eyes turned, as if in supplication, towards the vaulted ceiling.

"Have you got it?" asked Abdul.

"Yes."

"And what do we owe, adding it all together?"

"Forty billion dollars," said Toomuch.

"Isn't that wonderful!" exclaimed Abdul, with delight radiating over his countenance. "Who would have thought that before the war! Forty billion dollars! Aren't we the financiers! Aren't we the bulwark of monetary power! Can you touch that in Canada?"

"No," I said, "we can't. We don't owe two billion yet."

"Oh, never mind, never mind," said the little man in a consoling tone. "You are only a young country yet. You'll do better later on. And in any case I am sure you are just as proud of your one billion as we are of our forty."

"Oh, yes," I said, "we certainly are."

"Come, come, that's something anyway. You're on the right track, and you must not be discouraged if you're not up to the Turkish standard yet. You must remember, as I told you before, that Turkey leads the world in all ideas of government and finance. Take the present situation. Here we are, bankrupt--pass me the champagne, Toomuch, and sit down with us--the very first nation of the lot. It's a great feather in the cap of our financiers. It gives us a splendid start for the new era of reconstruction that we are beginning on. As you perhaps have heard we are all hugely busy about it. You notice my books and papers, do you not?" the Sultan added very proudly, waving his hand towards a great pile of blue books, pamphlets and documents that were heaped upon the floor beside him.

"Why! I never knew before that you ever read anything!" I exclaimed in amazement.

"Never did. But everything's changed now, isn't it, Toomuch? I sit and work here for hours every morning. It's become a delight to me. After all," said Abdul, lighting a big cigar and sticking up his feet on his pile of papers with an air of the deepest comfort, "what is there like work? So stimulating, so satisfying. I sit here working away, just like this, most of the day. There's nothing like it."

"What are you working at?" I asked.

"Reconstruction," said the little man, puffing a big cloud from his cigar, "reconstruction."

"What kind of reconstruction?"

"All kinds--financial, industrial, political, social. It's great stuff. By the way," he continued with great animation, "would you like to be my Minister of Labour? No? Well, I'm sorry. I half hoped you would. We're having no luck with them. The last one was thrown into the Bosphorous on Monday. Here's the report on it--no, that's the one on the shooting of the Minister of Religion--ah! here it is--Report on the Drowning of the Minister of Labour. Let me read you a bit of this: I call this one of the best reports, of its kind, that have come in."

"No, no," I said, "don't bother to read it. Just tell me who did it and why."

"Workingmen," said the Sultan, very cheerfully, "a delegation. They withheld their reasons."

"So you are having labour troubles here too?" I asked.

"Labour troubles!" exclaimed the little Sultan rolling up his eyes. "I should say so. The whole of Turkey is bubbling with labour unrest like the rosewater in a narghile. Look at your tablets, Toomuch, and tell me what new strikes there have been this morning."

The aged Secretary fumbled with his notes and began to murmur--"Truly will I try with the aid of Allah--"

"Now, now," said Abdul, warningly, "that won't do. Say simply 'Sure.' Now tell me."

The Secretary looked at a little list and read: "The strikes of to-day comprise--the wig-makers, the dog fanciers, the conjurers, the snake charmers, and the soothsayers."

"You hear that," said Abdul proudly. "That represents some of the most skilled labour in Turkey."

"I suppose it does," I said, "but tell me Abdul--what about the really necessary trades, the coal miners, the steel workers, the textile operatives, the farmers, and the railway people. Are they working?"

The little Sultan threw himself back on his cushions in a paroxysm of laughter, in which even his ancient Secretary was feign to join.

"My dear sir, my dear sir!" he laughed, "don't make me die of laughter. Working! those people working! Surely you don't think we are so behind hand in Turkey as all that! All those worker's stopped absolutely months ago. It is doubtful if they'll ever work again. There's a strong movement in Turkey to abolish all NECESSARY work altogether."

"But who then," I asked, "is working?"

"Look on the tablets, Toomuch, and see."

The aged Secretary bowed, turned over the leaves of his "tablets," which I now perceived on a closer view to be merely an American ten cent memorandum book. Then he read:

"The following, O all highest, still work--the beggars, the poets, the missionaries, the Salvation Army, and the instructors of the Youths of Light in the American Presbyterian College."

"But, dear me, Abdul," I exclaimed, "surely this situation is desperate? What can your nation subsist on in such a situation?"

"Pooh, pooh," said the Sultan. "The interest on our debt alone is two billion a year. Everybody in Turkey, great or small, holds bonds to some extent. At the worst they can all live fairly well on the interest. This is finance, is it not, Toomuch Koffi?"

"The very best and latest," said the aged man with a profound salaam.

"But what steps are you taking," I asked, "to remedy your labour troubles?"

"We are appointing commissions," said Abdul. "We appoint one for each new labour problem. How many yesterday, Toomuch?"

"Forty-three," answered the secretary.

"That's below our average, is it not?" said Abdul a little anxiously. "Try to keep it up to fifty if you can."

"And these commissions, what do they do?"

"They make Reports," said Abdul, beginning to yawn as if the continued brain exercise of conversation were fatiguing his intellect, "excellent reports. We have had some that are said to be perfect models of the very best Turkish." "And what do they recommend?"

"I don't know," said the Sultan. "We don't read them for that. We like to read them simply as Turkish."

"But what," I urged, "do you do with them? What steps do you take?"

"We send them all," replied the little man, puffing at his pipe and growing obviously drowsy as he spoke, "to Woodrow Wilson. He can deal with them. He is the great conciliator of the world. Let him have--how do you say it in English, it is a Turkish phrase--let him have his stomach full of conciliation."

Abdul dozed on his cushions for a moment. Then he reopened his eyes. "Is there anything else you want to know," he asked, "before I retire to the Inner Harem?"

"Just one thing," I said, "if you don't mind. How do you stand internationally? Are you coming into the New League of Nations?"

The Sultan shook his head.

"No," he said, "we're not coming in. We are starting a new league of our own."

"And who are in it?"

"Ourselves, and the Armenians--and let me see--the Irish, are they not, Toomuch--and the Bulgarians--are there any others, Toomuch?"

"There is talk," said the Secretary "of the Yugo-Hebrovians and the Scaroovians--"

"Who are they?" I asked.

"We don't know," said Abdul, testily. "They wrote to us. They seem all right. Haven't you got a lot of people in your league that you never heard of?"

"I see," I said, "and what is the scheme that your league is formed on?"

"Very simple," said the Sultan. "Each member of the league gives its WORD to all the other members. Then they all take an OATH together. Then they all sign it. That is absolutely binding."

He rolled back on his cushions in an evident state of boredom and weariness.

"But surely," I protested, "you don't think that a league of that sort can keep the peace?"

"Peace!" exclaimed Abdul waking into sudden astonishment. "Peace! I should think NOT! Our league is for WAR. Every member gives its word that at the first convenient opportunity it will knock the stuff out of any of the others that it can."

The little Sultan again subsided. Then he rose, with some difficulty, from his cushions.

"Toomuch," he said, "take our inquisitive friend out into the town; take him to the Bosphorous; take him to the island where the dogs are; take him anywhere." He paused to whisper a few instructions into the ear of the Secretary. "You understand," he said, "well, take him. As for me,"--he gave a great yawn as he shuffled away, "I am about to withdraw into my Inner Harem. Goodbye. I regret that I cannot invite you in."

"So do I," I said. "Goodbye."

IV.--Echoes of the War

1.--The Boy Who Came Back

The war is over. The soldiers are coming home. On all sides we are assured that the problem of the returned soldier is the gravest of our national concerns.

So I may say it without fear of contradiction,--since everybody else has seen it,--that, up to the present time, the returned soldier is a disappointment. He is not turning out as he ought. According to all the professors of psychology he was to come back bloodthirsty and brutalised, soaked in militarism and talking only of slaughter. In fact, a widespread movement had sprung up, warmly supported by the business men of the cities, to put him on the land. It was thought that central Nevada or northern Idaho would do nicely for him. At the same time an agitation had been started among the farmers, with the slogan "Back to the city," the idea being that farm life was so rough that it was not fair to ask the returned soldier to share it.

All these anticipations turn out to be quite groundless.

The first returned soldier of whom I had direct knowledge was my nephew Tom. When he came back, after two years in the trenches, we asked him to dine with us. "Now, remember," I said to my wife, "Tom will be a very different being from what he was when he went away. He left us as little more than a school boy, only in his first year at college; in fact, a mere child. You remember how he used to bore us with baseball talk and that sort of thing. And how shy he was! You recall his awful fear of Professor Razzler, who used to teach him mathematics. All that, of course, will be changed now. Tom will have come back a man. We must ask the old professor to meet him. It will amuse Tom to see him again. Just think of the things he must have seen! But we must be a little careful at dinner not to let him horrify the other people with brutal details of the war."

Tom came. I had expected him to arrive in uniform with his pocket full of bombs. Instead of this he wore ordinary evening dress with a dinner jacket. I realised as I helped him to take off his overcoat in the hall that he was very proud of his dinner jacket. He had never had one before. He said he wished the "boys" could see him in it. I asked him why he had put off his lieutenant's uniform so quickly. He explained that he was entitled not to wear it as soon as he had his discharge papers signed; some of the fellows, he said, kicked them off as soon as they left the ship, but the rule was, he told me, that you had to wear the thing till your papers were signed.

Then his eye caught a glimpse sideways of Professor Razzler standing on the hearth rug in the drawing room. "Say," he said, "is that the professor?" I could see that Tom was scared. All the signs of physical fear were written on his face. When I tried to lead him into the drawing room I realised that he was as shy as ever. Three of the women began talking to him all at once. Tom answered, yes or no,--with his eyes down. I liked the way he stood, though, so unconsciously erect and steady. The other men who came in afterwards, with easy greetings and noisy talk, somehow seemed loud-voiced and self-assertive.

Tom, to my surprise, refused a cocktail. It seems, as he explained, that he "got into the way of taking nothing over there." I noticed that my friend Quiller, who is a war correspondent, or, I should say, a war editorial writer, took three cocktails and talked all the more brilliantly for it through the opening courses of the dinner, about the story of the smashing of the Hindenburg line. He decided, after his second Burgundy, that it had been simply a case of sticking it out. I say "Burgundy" because we had substituted Burgundy, the sparkling kind, for champagne at our dinners as one of our little war economies.

Tom had nothing to say about the Hindenburg line. In fact, for the first half of the dinner he hardly spoke. I think he was worried about his left hand. There is a deep furrow across the back of it where a piece of shrapnel went through and there are two fingers that will hardly move at all. I could see that he was ashamed of its clumsiness and afraid that someone might notice it. So he kept silent. Professor

Razzler did indeed ask him straight across the table what he thought about the final breaking of the Hindenburg line. But he asked it with that same fierce look from under his bushy eyebrows with which he used to ask Tom to define the path of a tangent, and Tom was rattled at once. He answered something about being afraid that he was not well posted, owing to there being so little chance over there to read the papers.

After that Professor Razzler and Mr. Quiller discussed for us, most energetically, the strategy of the Lorraine sector (Tom served there six months, but he never said so) and high explosives and the possibilities of aerial bombs. (Tom was "buried" by an aerial bomb but, of course, he didn't break in and mention it.)

But we did get him talking of the war at last, towards the end of the dinner; or rather, the girl sitting next to him did, and presently the rest of us found ourselves listening. The strange thing was that the girl was a mere slip of a thing, hardly as old as Tom himself. In fact, my wife was almost afraid she might be too young to ask to dinner: girls of that age, my wife tells me, have hardly sense enough to talk to men, and fail to interest them. This is a proposition which I think it better not to dispute.

But at any rate we presently realized that Tom was talking about his war experiences and the other talk about the table was gradually hushed into listening.

This, as nearly as I can set it down, is what he told us: That the French fellows picked up baseball in a way that is absolutely amazing; they were not much good, it seems, at the bat, at any rate not at first, but at running bases they were perfect marvels; some of the French made good pitchers, too; Tom knew a poilu who had lost his right arm who could pitch as good a ball with his left as any man on the American side; at the port where Tom first landed and where they trained for a month they had a dandy ball ground, a regular peach, a former parade ground of the French barracks. On being asked WHICH port it was, Tom said he couldn't remember; he thought it was either Boulogne or Bordeaux or Brest,--at any rate, it was one of those places on the English channel. The ball ground they had behind the trenches was not so good; it was too much cut up by long range shells. But the ball ground at the base hospital (where Tom was sent for his second wound) was an A1 ground. The French doctors, it appears, were perfectly rotten at baseball, not a bit like the soldiers. Tom wonders that they kept them. Tom says that baseball had been tried among the German prisoners, but they are perfect dubs. He doubts whether the Germans will ever be able to play ball. They lack the national spirit. On the other hand, Tom thinks that the English will play a great game when they really get into it. He had two weeks' leave in London and went to see the game that King George was at, and says that the King, if they will let him, will make the greatest rooter of the whole bunch.

Such was Tom's war talk.

It grieved me to note that as the men sat smoking their cigars and drinking liqueur whiskey (we have cut out port at our house till the final peace is signed) Tom seemed to have subsided into being only a boy again, a first-year college boy among his seniors. They spoke to him in quite a patronising way, and even asked him two or three direct questions about fighting in the trenches, and wounds and the dead men in No Man's Land and the other horrors that the civilian mind hankers to hear about. Perhaps they thought, from the boy's talk, that he had seen nothing. If so, they were mistaken. For about three minutes, not more, Tom gave them what was coming to them. He told them, for example, why he trained his "fellows" to drive the bayonet through the stomach and not through the head, that the bayonet driven through the face or skull sticks and,--but there is no need to recite it here. Any of the boys like Tom can tell it all to you, only they don't want to and don't care to.

They've got past it.

But I noticed that as the boy talked,--quietly and reluctantly enough,--the older men fell silent and looked into his face with the realisation that behind his simple talk and quiet manner lay an inward vision of grim and awful realities that no words could picture.

I think that they were glad when we joined the ladies again and when Tom talked of the amateur vaudeville show that his company had got up behind the trenches.

Later on, when the other guests were telephoning for their motors and calling up taxis, Tom said he'd walk to his hotel; it was only a mile and the light rain that was falling would do him, he said, no harm at all. So he trudged off, refusing a lift.

Oh, no, I don't think we need to worry about the returned soldier. Only let him return, that's all. When he does, he's a better man than we are, Gunga Dinn.

2.--The War Sacrifices of Mr. Spugg

Although we had been members of the same club for years, I only knew Mr. Spugg by sight until one afternoon when I heard him saying that he intended to send his chauffeur to the war.

It was said quite quietly,--no bombast or boasting about it. Mr. Spugg was standing among a little group of listening members of the club and when he said that he had decided to send his chauffeur, he spoke with a kind of simple earnestness, a determination that marks the character of the man.

"Yes," he said, "we need all the man power we can command. This thing has come to a showdown and we've got to recognise it. I told Henry that it's a showdown and that he's to get ready and start right away."

"Well, Spugg," said one of the members "you're certainly setting us a fine example."

"What else can a man do?" said Mr. Spugg.

"When does your chauffeur leave?" asked another man.

"Right away. I want him in the firing line just as quick as I can get him there."

"It's a fine thing you're doing, Spugg," said a third member, "but do you realise that your chauffeur may be killed?"

"I must take my chance on that," answered Mr. Spugg, firmly. "I've thought this thing out and made up my mind: If my chauffeur is killed, I mean to pay for him,--full and adequate compensation. The loss must fall on me, not on him. Or, say Henry comes back mutilated,--say he loses a leg,--say he loses two legs,--"

Here Mr. Spugg looked about him at his listeners, with a look that meant that even three legs wouldn't be too much for him.

"Whatever Henry loses I pay for. The loss shall fall on me, every cent of it."

"Spugg," said a quiet looking, neatly dressed man whom I knew to be the president of an insurance company and who reached out and shook the speaker by the hand, "this is a fine thing you're doing, a big thing. But we mustn't let you do it alone. Let our company take a hand in it. We're making a special rate now on chauffeurs, footmen, and house-servants sent to the war, quite below the rate that actuarial figures justify. It is our little war contribution," he added modestly. "We like to feel that we're doing our bit, too. We had a chauffeur killed last week. We paid for him right off without demur,--waived all question of who killed him. I never signed a check (as I took occasion to say in a little note I wrote to his people) with greater pleasure."

"What do you do if Henry's mutilated?" asked Mr. Spugg, turning his quiet eyes on the insurance man and facing the brutal facts of things without flinching. "What do you pay? Suppose I lose the use of Henry's legs, what then?"

"It's all right," said his friend. "Leave it to us. Whatever he loses, we make it good."

"All right," said Spugg, "send me round a policy. I'm going to see Henry clear through on this."

It was at this point that at my own urgent request I was introduced to Mr. Spugg, so that I might add my congratulations to those of the others. I told him that I felt, as all the other members of the club did, that he was doing a big thing, and he answered again, in his modest way, that he didn't see what else a man could do.

"My son Alfred and I," he said, "talked it over last night and we agreed that we can run the car ourselves, or make a shot at it anyway. After all, it's war time."

"What branch of the service are you putting your chauffeur in?" I asked.

"I'm not sure," he answered. "I think I'll send him up in the air. It's dangerous, of course, but it's no time to think about that."

So, in due time, Mr. Spugg's chauffeur, Henry, went overseas. He was reported first as in England. Next he was right at the front, at the very firing itself. We knew then,--everybody in the club knew that Mr. Spugg's chauffeur might be killed at any moment. But great as the strain must have been, Spugg went up and down to his office and in and out of the club without a tremor. The situation gave him a new importance in our eyes, something tense.

"This seems to be a terrific business," I said to him one day at lunch, "this new German drive."

"My chauffeur," said Mr. Spugg, "was right in the middle of it."

"He was, eh?"

"Yes," he continued, "one shell burst in the air so near him it almost broke his wings."

Mr. Spugg told this with no false boasting or bravado, eating his celery as he spoke of it. Here was a man who had nearly had his chauffeur's wings blown off and yet he never moved a muscle. I began to realize the kind of resolute stuff that the man was made of.

A few days later bad news came to the club.

"Have you heard the bad news about Spugg?" someone asked.

"No, what?"

"His chauffeur's been gassed."

"How is he taking it?"

"Fine. He's sending off his gardener to take the chauffeur's place."

So that was Mr. Spugg's answer to the Germans.

We lunched together that day.

"Yes," he said, "Henry's gassed. How it happened I don't know. He must have come down out of the air. I told him I wanted him in the air. But let it pass. It's done now."

"And you're sending your gardener?"

"I am," said Spugg. "He's gone already. I called him in from the garden yesterday. I said, 'William, Henry's been gassed. Our first duty is to keep up our man power at the front. You must leave to-night.'"

"What are you putting William into?" I asked

"Infantry. He'll do best in the trenches,--digs well and is a very fair shot. Anyway I want him to see all the fighting that's going. If the Germans want give and take in this business they can have it. They'll soon see who can stand it best. I told William when he left. I said, 'William, we've got to show these fellows that man for man we're a match for them.' That's the way I look at it, man for man."

I watched Mr. Spugg's massive face as he went on with his meal. Not a nerve of it moved. If he felt any fear, at least he showed no trace of it.

After that I got war news from him at intervals, in little scraps, as I happened to meet him. "The war looks bad," I said to him one day as I chanced upon him getting into his motor. "This submarine business is pretty serious."

"It is," he said, "William was torpedoed yesterday."

Then he got into his car and drove away, as quietly as if nothing had happened.

A little later that day I heard him talking about it in the club. "Yes," he was say-ing, "a submarine. It torpedoed William,--my gardener. I have both a chauffeur and a gardener at the war. William was picked up on a raft. He's in pretty bad shape. My son Alfred had a cable from him that he's coming home. We've both telegraphed him to stick it out."

The news was the chief topic in the club that day. "Spugg's gardener has been torpedoed," they said, "but Spugg refuses to have him quit and come home." "Well done, Spugg," said everybody.

After that we had news from time to time about both William and Henry.

"Henry's out of the hospital," said Spugg. "I hope to have him back in France in a few days. William's in bad shape still. I had a London surgeon go and look at him. I told him not to mind the expense but to get William fixed up right away. It seems that one arm is more or less paralysed. I've wired back to him not to hesitate. They say William's blood is still too thin for the operation. I've cabled to them to take some of Henry's. I hate to do it, but this is no time to stick at anything."

A little later William and Henry were reported both back in France. This was at the very moment of the great offensive. But Spugg went about his daily business unmoved. Then came the worst news of all. "William and Henry," he said to me, "are both missing. I don't know where the devil they are."

"Missing?" I repeated.

"Both of them. The Germans have caught them both. I suppose I shan't have either of them back now till the war is all over."

He gave a slight sigh,--the only sign of complaint that ever I had heard come from him.

But the next day we learned what was Spugg's answer to the German's capture of William and Henry.

"Have you heard what Spugg is doing?" the members of the club asked one another.

"What?"

"He's sending over Meadows, HIS OWN MAN!"

There was no need to comment on it. The cool courage of the thing spoke for itself. Meadows,--Spugg's own man,--his house valet, without whom he never trav-elled twenty miles!

"What else was there to do?" said Mr. Spugg when I asked him if it was true that Meadows was going. "I take no credit for sending Meadows nor, for the matter of that, for anything that Meadows may do over there. It was a simple matter of duty. My son and I had him into the dining room last night after dinner. 'Meadows,' we said, 'Henry and William are caught. Our man power at the front has got to be kept up. There's no one left but ourselves and you. There's no way out of it. You'll have to go.'"

"But how," I protested, "can you get along with Meadows, your valet, gone? You'll be lost!"

"We must do the best we can. We've talked it all over. My son will help me dress and I will help him. We can manage, no doubt."

So Meadows went.

After this Mr. Spugg, dressed as best he could manage it, and taking turns with his son in driving his own motor, was a pathetic but uncomplaining object.

Meadows meantime was reported as with the heavy artillery, doing well. "I hope nothing happens to Meadows," Spugg kept saying. "If it does, we're stuck. We can't go ourselves. We're too busy. We've talked it over and we've both decided that it's impossible to get away from the office,--not with business as brisk as it is now. We're busier than we've been in ten years and can't get off for a day. We may try to take a month off for the Adirondacks a little later but as for Europe, it's out of the question."

Meantime, one little bit of consolation came to help Mr. Spugg to bear the burden of the war. I found him in the lounge room of the club one afternoon among a group of men, exhibiting two medals that were being passed from hand to hand.

"Sent to me by the French government," he explained proudly. "They're for William and Henry. The motto means, 'For Conspicuous Courage'" (Mr. Spugg drew himself up with legitimate pride). "I shall keep one and let Alfred keep the other till they come back." Then he added, as an afterthought, "They may never come back."

From that day on, Mr. Spugg, with his French medal on his watch chain, was the most conspicuous figure in the club. He was pointed out as having done more than any other one man in the institution to keep the flag flying. But presently the limit of Mr. Spugg's efforts and sacrifices was reached. Even patriotism such as his must have some bounds.

On entering the club one afternoon I could hear his voice bawling vociferously in one of the telephone cabinets in the hall. "Hello, Washington," he was shouting. "Is that Washington? Long Distance, I want Washington."

Fifteen minutes later he came up to the sitting room, still flushed with indignation and excitement. "That's the limit," he said, "the absolute limit!"

"What's the matter?" I asked.

"They drafted my son Alfred," he answered.

"Just imagine it! When we're so busy in the office that we're getting down there at half past eight in the morning! Drafted Alfred! 'Great Caesar' I said to them! 'Look here! You've had my chauffeur and he's gassed, and you've had my gardener and he's torpedoed and they're both prisoners, and last month I sent you my own man! That,' I said, 'is about the limit.'"

"What did they say," I asked.

"Oh, it's all right. They've fixed it all up and they've apologized as well. Alfred won't go, of course, but it makes one realise that you can carry a thing too far. Why, they'd be taking me next!"

"Oh, surely not!" I said.

3.--If Germany Had Won

Sometimes, in the past, we have grown a little impatient with our North American civilisation, with its strident clamour, its noisy elections, its extremes of liberty, its occasional corruption and the faults that we now see were the necessary accompaniments of its merits. But let us set beside it a picture such as this, taken from the New York Imperial Gazette of 1925--or from any paper of the same period, such as would have been published if Germany had won.

General Boob of Boobenstiff, Imperial Governor of New York, will attend divine (Imperial) service on Sunday morning next at the church of St. John the (Imperial) Divine. The subway cars will be stopped while the General is praying. All subway passengers are enjoined (befohlen), during the thus-to-be-ordered period of cessation, to remain in a reverential attitude. Those in the seats will keep the head bowed. Those holding to the straps will elevate one leg, keeping the knee in the air.

On Monday evening General Boob von Boobenstiff, Imperial Governor of New York, will be graciously pleased to attend a performance at the (Imperial) Winter Garden on Upper (Imperial) Broadway. It is ordered that on the entrance of His Excellency the audience will spontaneously rise and break into three successive enthusiastic cheers. Mr. Al Jolson will remain kneeling on the stage till the Gubernatorial All Highest has seated itself. Mr. Jolson will then, by special (Imperial) permission, be allowed to make four jokes in German to be taken from a list supplied by the Imperial Censor of Humour. The Governor, accompanied by his military staff, will then leave, and the performance will close.

It is ordered that, on Tuesday afternoon, as a sign of thankfulness for the blessings of the German peace, the business men of New York shall walk in procession from the Battery to the Bronx. They will then be inspected by Governor Boobenstiff. If the Governor is delayed in arriving at the hereafter-to-be-indicated point of general put-yourself-there, the procession will walk back to the Battery and back again, continuing so, pro and con, till the arrival of the Governor.

The approaching visit of His Royal and Imperial Solemnity the Prince Apparent of Bavaria shall be heralded in the (Imperial) City of New York with general rejoicing. The city shall be spontaneously decorated with flags. Smiles of cordial welcome shall appear on every face. Animated crowds of eager citizens shall move to and fro and shouts of welcome shall, by order of the Chief of Police, break from the lips. Among those who are expected to be in the Imperial city to welcome his Royal Solemnity will be the Hereditary Grand Duke of Schlitzin-Mein (formerly Milwaukee), the Prince Margrave of Wisconsin and the Hereditary Chief Constable of Nevada.

We are delighted to be able to chronicle that on the morning of the 14th there was born at the Imperial Residence of His Simplicity the Hereditary Governor of the Provinz (formerly State) of New York, in the (Imperial) city of Albany a tenth son to the illustrious Prince and Princess who rule over us with such fatherly care. The boy was christened yesterday at the (Imperial) Lutheran Church and is to bear the name Frederick Wilhelm Amelia Mary Johan Heinrich Ruprecht. The whole city of Albany is thrown into the wildest rejoicing. The legislature has voted an addition of $400,000 per annum to the civil list for the maintenance of the young prince. Joy suffuses every home. This being the tenth son born to their Highnesses in ten years it is felt that the future of the dynasty is more or less secured. Even the humblest home is filled with the reflected joy that streams out from the Residency. Their Royal Highnesses appeared yesterday on the balcony amid the wild huzzoos of the people transported with joy. His Simplicity the Prince wore the full dress uniform of an Imperial Jaeger of the Adirondacks, and Her Royal Highness was attired as a Colonel of Artillery. It is impossible to express the jubilation of the moment.

We regret to report that owing to the jostling (possibly accidental, but none the less actual) of an Imperial officer--Field-Lieutenant Schmidt--at the entrance to Brooklyn Bridge, the bridge is declared closed to the public until further notice. We are proud to state the Field Lieutenant at once cut down his cowardly assailant with his saber. It has pleased His Unspeakable Loftiness, the German Emperor, to cable his congratulations to the Lieutenant, who will receive The Order of the Dead Dog for the noble way in which he has maintained the traditions of his uniform.

A striking feature of the now-taking-place Art Exhibition at the Kaiser Wilhelm Institute (formerly Metropolitan Gallery) in the Thiergarten (formerly Central Park) is offered by the absolutely marvellous paintings exhibited by the Princess Marie Paul Cecilie Hohenzollern-Stickitintothem, a cousin of Our Noble Governor. The paintings which the Princess has been preciously pleased to paint and has even stooped to exhibit to the filled-with-wonder eye of the public have been immediately awarded the first prize in each class. While it would be invidious even to suggest that any one of Her High Incipiency's pictures is better than any other, our feeling is that especially the picture Night on the Hudson River is of so rare a quality both of technique and of inspiration that it supersedes the bounds of the hitherto-thought-to-be-possible art in America. The Princess's conception of night, black as a pall and yet luminous as a polished stove pipe, is only equalled by her feeling towards the Hudson which lies extended in soporific superficiality beneath the sable covering of darkness in which Her Highness has been pleased to overwhelm it. Throughout the day an eager-to-see crowd of spectators were beaten back from the picture by the police with clubs.

We are permitted officially to confirm the already gladly-from-mouth-to-mouth-whispered news of an approaching marriage between Prince Heinrich of Texas and the Princess Amelia Victoria Louisa, Hereditary Heir Consumptive of the Imperial Provinz of Maine. The marriage, so it is whispered, although performed in accordance with the wishes of the Emperor as expressed by cable, is in every way a love match. What lends a touch of romance to the betrothal of the Royal Young-lings is that the Prince had never even seen the Princess Amelia until the day when the legislature of the Provinz of Maine voted her a marriage portion of half a million dollars. Immediately on this news a secret visit was arranged, the Prince journeying to Bangor incognito as the Count of Flim-Flam in the costume of an officer of the Imperial Scavengers. On receipt of the Emperor's telegram the happy pair fell in love with one another at once. What makes the approaching union particularly auspicious for the whole country is that it brings with it the union of Maine and Texas, henceforth to form a single grateful provinz. The Royal Pair, it is understood, will live alternately in each province a month at a time and the legislature, the executive officials, the courts of law and the tax collectors will follow them to and fro.

We cannot but contrast this happy issue with the turbulence and disorder in which our country lived before the Great War of Liberation.

We are delighted to learn from our despatches from Boston that the Hohen-zollern Institute (formerly Harvard University) is to be opened next autumn. By express permission of the Imperial Government, classes in English will be permitted for half an hour each day.

By the clemency of the Emperor the sentences of W. H. Taft, and W. Wilson have been commuted from the sentence of fifty years imprisonment to imprison-ment for life. We hope, in a special supplement, to be able to add the full list of sentences, executions, imprisonments, fines, and attainders that have been promul-gated in honour of the birthday of our Imperial Sovereign.

4.--War and Peace at the Galaxy Club

The Great Peace Kermesse at the Galaxy Club, to which I have the honour to belong, held with a view to wipe out the Peace Deficit of the Club, has just ended. For three weeks our club house has been a blaze of illumination. We have had four orchestras in attendance. There have been suppers and dances every night. Our members have not spared themselves.

The Kermesse is now over. We have time, as our lady members are saying, to turn round.

For the moment we are sitting listening, amid bursts of applause, to our treasurer's statement. As we hear it we realise that this Peace Kermesse has proved the culmination and crown of four winters' war work.

But I must explain from the beginning.

Our efforts began with the very opening of the war. We felt that a rich organisation like ours ought to do something for the relief of the Belgians. At the same time we felt that our members would rather receive something in the way of entertainment for their money than give it straight out of their pockets.

We therefore decided first to hold a public lecture in the club, and engaged the services of Professor Dry to lecture on the causes of the war.

In view of the circumstances, Professor Dry very kindly reduced his lecture fee, which (he assured us) is generally two hundred and fifty dollars, to two hundred and forty.

The lecture was most interesting. Professor Dry traced the causes of the War backwards through the Middle Ages. He showed that it represented the conflict of the brachiocephalic culture of the Wendic races with the dolichocephalic culture of the Alpine stock. At the time when the lights went out he had got it back to the eighth century before Christ.

Unfortunately the night, being extremely wet, was unfavourable. Few of our members care to turn out to lectures in wet weather. The treasurer was compelled to announce to the Committee a net deficit of two hundred dollars. Some of the ladies of the Committee moved that the entire deficit be sent to the Belgians, but were overruled by the interference of the men.

But the error was seen to have been in the choice of the lecturer. Our members were no longer interested in the causes of the war. The topic was too old. We therefore held another public lecture in the club, on the topic What Will Come After the War. It was given by a very talented gentleman, a Mr. Guess, a most interesting speaker, who reduced his fee (as the thing was a war charity) by one-half, leaving it at three hundred dollars. Unhappily the weather was against us. It was too fine. Our members scarcely care to listen to lectures in fine weather. And it turned out that our members are not interested in what will come after the war. The topic is too new. Our receipts of fifty dollars left us with a net deficit of two hundred and fifty. Our treasurer therefore proposed that we should carry both deficits forward and open a Special Patriotic Entertainment Account showing a net total deficit of four hundred and fifty dollars.

In the opinion of the committee our mistake had been in engaging outside talent. It was felt that the cost of this was prohibitive. It was better to invite the services of the members of the club themselves. A great number of the ladies expressed their willingness to take part in any kind of war work that took the form of public entertainment.

Accordingly we presented a play. It was given in the ball room of the club house, a stage being specially put up for us by a firm of contractors. The firm (as a matter of patriotism) did the whole thing for us at cost, merely charging us with the labour, the material, the time, the thought and the anxiety that they gave to the job, but for nothing else. In fact, the whole staging, including lights, plumbing and decorations was merely a matter of five hundred dollars. The plumbers very considerately made no charge for their time, but only for their work.

It was felt that it would be better to have a new play than an old. We selected a brilliant little modern drawing-room comedy never yet presented. The owner of the copyright, a theatrical firm, let us use it for a merely nominal fee of two hundred dollars, including the sole right to play the piece forever. There being only twenty-eight characters in it, it was felt to be more suitable than a more ambitious thing. The tickets were placed at one dollar, no one being admitted free except the performers themselves, and the members who very kindly acted as scene shifters, curtain lifters, ushers, door-keepers, programme sellers, and the general committee of management. All the performers, at their own suggestion, supplied their own costumes, charging nothing to the club except the material and the cost of dressmaking. Beyond this there was no expense except for the fee, very reasonable, of Mr. Skip, the professional coach who trained the performers, and who asked us, in view of the circumstances, less than half of what he would have been willing to accept.

The proceeds were to be divided between the Belgian Fund and the Red Cross, giving fifty per cent to each. A motion in amendment from the ladies' financial committee to give fifty per cent to the Belgian Fund and sixty per cent to the Red Cross was voted down.

Unfortunately it turned out that the idea of a PLAY was a mistake in judgment. Our members, it seemed, did not care to go to see a play except in a theatre. A great number of them, however, very kindly turned out to help in shifting the scenery and in acting as ushers.

Our treasurer announced, as the result of the play, a net deficit of twelve hundred dollars. He moved, with general applause, that it be carried forward.

The total deficit having now reached over sixteen hundred dollars, there was a general feeling that a very special effort must be made to remove it. It was decided to hold Weekly Patriotic Dances in the club ball room, every Saturday evening. No charge was made for admission to the dances, but a War Supper was served at one dollar a head.

Unfortunately the dances, as first planned, proved again an error. It appeared that though our members are passionately fond of dancing, few if any of them cared to eat at night. The plan was therefore changed. The supper was served first, and was free, and for the dancing after supper a charge was made of one dollar, per person. This again was an error. It seems that after our members have had supper they prefer to go home and sleep. After one winter of dancing the treasurer announced a total Patriotic Relief Deficit of five thousand dollars, to be carried forward to next year. This sum duly appeared in the annual balance sheet of the club. The members, especially the ladies, were glad to think that we were at least doing SOMETHING for the war.

At this point some of our larger men, themselves financial experts, took hold. They said that our entertainments had been on too small a scale. They told us that we had been "undermined by overhead expenses." The word "overhead" was soon on everybody's lips. We were told that if we could "distribute our overhead" it would disappear. It was therefore planned to hold a great War Kermesse with a view to spreading out the overhead so thin that it would vanish.

But it was at this very moment that the Armistice burst upon us in a perfectly unexpected fashion. Everyone of our members was, undoubtedly, delighted that the war was over but there was a very general feeling that it would have been better if we could have had a rather longer notice of what was coming. It seemed, as many of our members said, such a leap in the dark to rush into peace all at once. It was said indeed by our best business men that in financial circles they had been fully aware that there was a danger of peace for some time and had taken steps to discount the peace risk.

But for the club itself the thing came with a perfect crash. The whole preparation of the great Kermesse was well under way when the news broke upon us. For a time the members were aghast. It looked like ruin. But presently it was suggested that it might still be possible to save the club by turning the whole affair into a Peace Kermesse and devoting the proceeds to some suitable form of relief. Luckily it was discovered that there was still a lot of starvation in Russia, and fortunately it turned out that in spite of the armistice the Turks were still killing the Armenians.

So it was decided to hold the Kermesse and give all the profits realised by it to the Victims of the Peace. Everybody set to work again with a will. The Kermesse indeed had to be postponed for a few months to make room for the changes needed, but it has now been held and, in a certain sense, it has been the wildest kind of success. The club, as I said, has been a blaze of light for three weeks. We have had four orchestras in attendance every evening. There have been booths draped with the flags of all the Allies, except some that we were not sure about, in every corridor of the club. There have been dinner parties and dances every evening. The members, especially the ladies, have not spared themselves. Many of them have spent practically all their time at the Kermesse, not getting home until two in the morning.

And yet somehow one has felt that underneath the surface it was not a success. The spirit seemed gone out of it. The members themselves confessed in confidence that in spite of all they could do their hearts were not in it. Peace had somehow taken away all the old glad sense of enjoyment. As to spending money at the Kermesse all the members admitted frankly that they had no heart for it. This was especially the case when the rumour got abroad that the Armenians were a poor lot and that some of the Turks were quite gentlemanly fellows. It was said, too, that if the Russians did starve it would do them a lot of good.

So it was known even before we went to hear the financial report that there would be no question of profits on the Kermesse going to the Armenians or the Russians.

And to-night the treasurer has been reading out to a general meeting the financial results as nearly as they can be computed.

He has put the Net Patriotic Deficit, as nearly as he can estimate it, at fifteen thousand dollars, though he has stated, with applause from the ladies, that the Gross Deficit is bigger still.

The Ladies Financial Committee has just carried a motion that the whole of the deficit, both net and gross, be now forwarded to the Red Cross Society (sixty per cent), the Belgian Relief Fund (fifty per cent), and the remainder invested in the War Loan.

But there is a very general feeling among the male members that the club will have to go into liquidation. Peace has ruined us. Not a single member, so far as I am aware, is prepared to protest against the peace, or is anything but delighted to think that the war is over. At the same time we do feel that if we could have had a longer notice, six months for instance, we could have braced ourselves better to stand up against it and meet the blow when it fell.

I think, too, that our feeling is shared outside.

5.--The War News as I Remember it

Everybody, I think, should make some little contribution towards keeping alive the memories of the great war. In the larger and heroic sense this is already being done. But some of the minor things are apt to be neglected. When the record of the war has been rewritten into real history, we shall be in danger of forgetting what WAR NEWS was like and the peculiar kind of thrill that accompanied its perusal.

Hence in order to preserve it for all time I embalm some little samples of it, selected of course absolutely at random,--as such things always are--in the pages of this book.

Let me begin with:--

I--THE CABLE NEWS FROM RUSSIA

This was the great breakfast-table feature for at least three years. Towards the end of the war some people began to complain of it. They said that they questioned whether it was accurate. Here for example is one fortnight of it.

Petrograd, April 14. Word has reached here that the
Germans have captured enormous quantities of grain on
the Ukrainian border. April 15. The Germans have captured no grain on the
Ukrainian border. The country is swept bare. April 16. Everybody in Petrograd is starving. April 17. There is no lack of food in Petrograd. April 18. The death of General Korniloff is credibly
reported this morning. April 19. It is credibly reported this morning that
General Korniloff is alive. April 20. It is credibly reported that General
Korniloff is hovering between life and death. April 21. The Bolsheviki are over-thrown. April 22. The Bolsheviki got up again. April 23. The Czar died last night. April 24. The Czar did not die last night. April 25. General Kaleidescope and his Cossacks
are moving north. April 26. General Kaleidescope and his Cossacks
are moving south. April 27. General Kaleidescope and his Cossacks
are moving east. April 28. General Kaleidescope and his Cossacks
are moving west. April 29. It is reported that the Cossacks under General
Kaleidescope have revolted. They demand the Maximum.
General Kaleidescope hasn't got it. April 30. The National Pan-Russian Con-stituent Universal
Duma which met this morning at ten-thirty, was
dissolved at twenty-five minutes to eleven.

My own conclusion, reached with deep regret, is that the Russians are not yet fit for the blessings of the Magna Carta and the Oklahoma Constitution of 1907.

They ought to remain for some years yet under the Interstate Commerce Commission.

II--SAMPLE OF SPECIAL CORRESPONDENCE

New York (through London via Holland and coming out at Madrid). Mr. O. Howe Lurid, our special correspondent, writing from "Somewhere near Somewhere" and describing the terrific operations of which he has just been an eyewitness, says:

"From the crest where I stood, the whole landscape about me was illuminated with the fierce glare of the bursting shells, while the ground on which I stood quivered with the thunderous detonation of the artillery.

"Nothing in the imagination of a Dante could have equalled the lurid and pyrogriffic grandeur of the scene. Streams of fire rose into the sky, falling in bifurcated crystallations in all directions. Disregarding all personal danger, I opened one eye and looked at it.

"I found myself now to be the very centre of the awful conflict. While not stating that the whole bombardment was directed at me personally, I am pretty sure that it was."

I admit that there was a time, at the very beginning of the war, when I liked this kind of thing served up with my bacon and eggs every morning, in the days when a man could eat bacon and eggs without being labelled a pro-German. Later on I came to prefer the simple statements as to the same scene and event, given out by Sir Douglas Haig and General Pershing--after this fashion:

"Last night at ten-thirty P.M. our men noticed signs of a light bombardment apparently coming from the German lines."

III--THE TECHNICAL WAR DESPATCHES

The best of these, as I remember them, used to come from the Italian front and were done after this fashion:--

"Tintino, near Trombono. Friday, April 3. The Germans, as I foresaw last month they would, have crossed the Piave in considerable force. Their position, as I said it would be, is now very strong. The mountains bordering the valley run--just as I foresaw they would--from northwest to southeast. The country in front is, as I anticipated, flat. Venice is, as I assured my readers it would be, about thirty miles distant from the Piave, which falls, as I expected it would, into the Adriatic."

IV--THE WAR PROPHECIES

Startling Prophecy in Paris. All Paris is wildly excited over the extraordinary prophecy of Madame Cleo de Clichy that the war will be over in four weeks. Madame Cleo, who is now as widely known as a diseuse, a liseuse, a friseuse and a clairvoyante, leaped into sudden prominence last November by her startling announcement that the seven letters in the Kaiser's name W i l h e l m represented the seven great beasts of the apocalypse; in the next month she electrified all Paris by her disclosure that the four letters of the word C z a r--by substituting the figure 1 for C, 9 for Z, 1 for A, and 7 for R produce the date 1917, and indicated a revolution in Russia. The salon of Madame Cleo is besieged by eager crowds night and day. She may prophesy again at any minute.

Startling Forecast. A Russian peasant, living in Semipalatinsk, has foretold that the war will end in August. The wildest excitement prevails not only in Semipalatinsk but in the whole of it.

Extraordinary Prophecy. Rumbumbabad, India. April 1. The whole neighbourhood has been thrown into a turmoil by the prophecy of Ram Slim, a Yogi of this district, who has foretold that the war will be at an end in September. People are pouring into Rumbumbabad in ox-carts from all directions. Business in Rumbumbabad is at a standstill.

Excitement in Midgeville, Ohio. William Bessemer Jones, a retired farmer of Cuyahoga, Ohio, has foretold that the war will end in October. People are flocking into Midgeville in lumber wagons from all parts of the country. Jones, who bases his prophecy on the Bible, had hitherto been thought to be half-witted. This is now recognised to have been a wrong estimate of his powers. Business in Midgeville is at a standstill.

Dog's Foot. Wyoming. April 1. An Indian of the Cheyenne tribe has foretold that the war will end in December. Business among the Indians is at a standstill.

V--DIPLOMATIC REVELATIONS

These were sent out in assortments, and labelled Vienna, via London, through Stockholm. After reading them with feverish eagerness for nearly four years, I decided that they somehow lack definiteness. Here is the way they ran:

"Special Correspondence. I learn from a very high authority, whose name I am not at liberty to mention, (speaking to me at a place which I am not allowed to indicate and in a language which I am forbidden to use)--that Austria-Hungary is about to take a diplomatic step of the highest importance. What this step is, I am forbidden to say. But the consequences of it--which unfortunately I am pledged not to disclose--will be such as to effect results which I am not free to enumerate."

VI--A NEW GERMAN PEACE FORMULA

Dr. Hertling, the Imperial Chancellor, speaking through his hat in the Reichstag, said that he wished to state in the clearest language of which he was capable that the German peace plan would not only provide the fullest self determination of all ethnographic categories, but would predicate the political self consciousness (politisches Selbstbewusztsein) of each geographical and entomological unit, subject only to the necessary rectilinear guarantees for the seismographic action of the German empire. The entire Reichstag, especially the professorial section of it, broke into unrestrained applause. It is felt that the new formula is the equivalent of a German Magna Carta--or as near to it as they can get.

VII--THE FINANCIAL NEWS

The war finance, as I remember it, always supplied items of the most absorbing interest. I do not mean to say that I was an authority on finance or held any official position in regard to it. But I watched it. I followed it in the newspapers. When the war began I knew nothing about it. But I picked up a little bit here and a little bit there until presently I felt that I had a grasp on it not easily shaken off.

It was a simple matter, anyway. Take the case of the rouble. It rose and it fell. But the reason was always perfectly obvious. The Russian news ran, as I got it in my newspapers, like this:--

"M. Touchusoff, the new financial secretary of the Soviet, has declared that Russia will repay her utmost liabilities. Roubles rose."

"M. Touchusoff, the late financial secretary of the Soviet, was thrown into the Neva last evening. Roubles fell."

"M. Gorky, speaking in London last night, said that Russia was a great country. Roubles rose."

"A Dutch correspondent, who has just beat his way out of Russia, reports that nothing will induce him to go back. Roubles fell."

"Mr. Arthur Balfour, speaking in the House of Commons last night, paid a glowing tribute to the memory of Peter the Great. Roubles rose."

"The local Bolsheviki of New York City at the Pan-Russian Congress held in Murphy's Rooms, Fourth Avenue, voted unanimously in favor of a Free Russia. Roubles never budged."

With these examples in view, anybody, I think, could grasp the central principles of Russian finance. All that one needed to know was what M. Touchusoff and such people were going to say, and who would be thrown into the Neva, and the rise and fall of the rouble could be foreseen to a kopeck. In speculation by shrewd people with proper judgment as to when to buy and when to sell the rouble, large fortunes could be made, or even lost, in a day.

But after all the Russian finance was simple. That of our German enemies was much more complicated and yet infinitely more successful. That at least I gathered from the little news items in regard to German finance that used to reach us in cables that were headed Via Timbuctoo and ran thus:--

"The fourth Imperial War Loan of four billion marks, to be known as the Kaiser's War Loan, was oversubscribed to-day in five minutes. Investors thronged the banks, with tears in their eyes, bringing with them everything that they had. The bank managers, themselves stained with tears, took everything that was offered. Each investor received a button proudly displayed by the too-happy-for-words out-of-the-bank-hustling recipient."

6.--Some Just Complaints About the War

No patriotic man would have cared to lift up his voice against the Government in war time. Personally, I should not want to give utterance even now to anything in the way of criticism. But the complaints which were presented below came to me, unsought and unsolicited, and represented such a variety of sources and such just and unselfish points of view that I think it proper, for the sake of history, to offer them to the public.

I give them, just as they reached me, without modifications of any sort.

The just complaint of Mr. Threadler, my tailor, as expressed while measuring me for my Win-the-War autumn suit.

"Complaint, sir? Oh, no, we have no complaint to make in our line of business, none whatever (forty-two, Mr. Jephson). It would hardly become us to complain (side pockets, Mr. Jephson). But we think, perhaps, it is rather a mistake for the Government (thirty-three on the leg) to encourage the idea of economy in dress. Our attitude is that the well dressed man (a little fuller in the chest? Yes, a little fuller in the chest, please, Mr. Jephson) is better able to serve his country than the man who goes about in an old suit. The motto of our trade is Thrift with Taste. It was made up in our spring convention of five hundred members, in a four day sitting. We feel it to be (twenty-eight) very appropriate. Our feeling is that a gentleman wearing one of our thrift worsteds under one of our Win-the-War light overcoats (Mr. Jephson, please show that new Win-the-War overcoating) is really helping to keep things going. We like to reflect, sir (nothing in shirtings, today?) that we're doing our bit, too, in presenting to the enemy an undisturbed nation of well dressed men. Nothing else, sir? The week after next? Ah! If we can, sir! but we're greatly rushed with our new and patriotic Thrift orders. Good morning, sir."

The just complaint of Madame Pavalucini, the celebrated contralto. As interviewed incidentally in the palm-room of The Slitz Hotel, over a cup of tea (one dollar), French Win-the-War pastry (one fifty) and Help-the-Navy cigarettes (fifty).

"I would not want to creetecize ze gouvermen' ah! non! That would be what you call a skonk treeck, hein?" (Madame Pavalucini comes from Missouri, and dares not talk any other kind of English than this, while on tour, with any strangers listening.) "But, I ask myself, ees it not just a leetle wrong to discourage and tax ze poor artistes? We are doing our beet, hein? We seeng, we recite! I seeng so many beautiful sings to ze soldiers; sings about love, and youth, and passion, and spring and kisses. And the men are carried off their feet. They rise. They rush to the war. I have seen them, in my patriotic concerts where I accept nothing but my expenses and my fee and give all that is beyond to the war. Only last night one arose, right in the front rank--the fauteuils d'orchestre, I do not know how you call them in English. 'Let me out of zis,' he scream, 'me for the war! Me for the trenches!' Was it not magnifique--what you call splendide, hein?

"And then ze gouvermen' come and tell me I must pay zem ten thousan' dollars, when I make only seexty thousan' dollars at ze opera! Anozzer skonk treeck, hein?"

The just complaint of Mr. Grunch, income tax payer, as imparted to me over his own port wine, after dinner.

"No, I shouldn't want to complain: I mean, in any way that would reach the outside,--reach it, that is, in connection with my name. Though I think that the thing ought to be said by SOMEBODY. I think you might say it. (Let me pour you out another glass of this Conquistador: yes, it's the old '87: but I suppose we'll never get any more of it on this side: they say that the rich Spaniards are making so much money they're buying up every cask of it and it will never be exported again. Just another illustration of the way that the war hits everybody alike.) But, as I was saying, I think if YOU were to raise a complaint about the income tax, you'd find the whole country--I mean all the men with incomes--behind you. I don't suppose they'd want you to mention their names. But they'd be BEHIND you, see? They'd all be there. (Will you try one of these Googoolias? They're the very best, but I guess we'll never see them again. They say the rich Cubans are buying them up. So the war hits us there, too.) As I see it, the income tax is the greatest mistake the government ever made. It hits the wrong man. It falls on the man with an income and lets the other man escape. The way I look at it, and the way all the men that will be behind you look at it, is that if a man sticks tight to it and goes on earning all the income he can, he's doing his bit, in his own way, to win the war. All we ask is to be let alone (don't put that in your notes as from me, but you can say it), let us alone to go on quietly piling up income till we get the Germans licked. But if you start to take away our income, you discourage us, you knock all the patriotism out of us. To my mind, a man's income and his patriotism are the same thing. But, of course, don't say that I said that."

The just complaint of my barber, as expressed in the pauses of his operations.

"I'm not saying nothing against the Government (any facial massage this morning?). I guess they know their own business, or they'd ought to, anyway. But I kick at all this talk against the barber business in war time (will I singe them ends a bit?). The papers are full of it, all the time. I don't see much else in them. Last week I saw where a feller said that all the barber shops ought to be closed up (bay rum?) till the war was over. Say, I'd like to have him right here in this chair with a razor at his throat, the way I have you! As I see it, the barber business is the most necessary business in the whole war. A man'll get along without everything else, just about, but he can't get along without a shave, can he?--or not without losing all the pep and self-respect that keeps him going. They say them fellers over in France has to shave every morning by military order: if they didn't the Germans would have 'em beat. I say the barber is doing his bit as much as any man. I was to Washington four months last winter, and I done all the work of three senators and two congressmen (will I clip that neck?) and I done the work of a United States Admiral every Saturday night. If that ain't war work, show me what is. But I don't kick, I just go along. If a man appreciates what I do, and likes to pay a little extra for it, why so much the better, but if he's low enough to get out of this chair you're in and walk off without giving a cent more than he has to, why let him go. But, sometimes, when I get thinking about all this outcry about barber's work in war time, I feel like following the man to the door and slitting his throat for him... Thank you, sir; thank you, sir. Good morning. Next!"

The just complaint of Mr. Singlestone;--formerly Mr. Einstein, Theatre Proprietor.

"I would be the last man, the very last, to say one word against the Government. I think they are doing fine. I think the boys in the trenches are doing fine. I think the nation is doing fine. But, if there's just one thing where they're wrong, it's in the matter of the theatres. I think it would be much better for the Government not to attempt to cut down or regulate theatres in any way. The theatre is the people's recreation. It builds them up. It's all part of a great machine to win the war. I like to stand in the box office and see the money come in and feel that the theatre is doing its bit. But, mind you, I think the President is doing fine. So, all I say is, I think the theatres ought to be allowed to do fine, too."

The just complaint of Mr. Silas Heck, farmer, as interviewed by me, incognito, at the counter of the Gold Dollar Saloon.

"Yes, sir, I say the Government's in the wrong, and I don't care who hears me. (Say, is that feller in the slick overcoat listening? Let's move along a little further.) They're right to carry on the war for all the nation is worth. That's sound and I'm with 'em. But they ought not to take the farmer offen his farm. There I'm agin them. The farmer is the one man necessary for the country. They say they want bacon for the Allies. Well, the way I look at it is, if you want bacon, you need hogs. And if there are no men left in the country like me, what'll you do for hogs!

"Thanks, was you paying for that? I guess we won't have another, eh? Two of them things might be bad for a feller."

So, when I used to listen to the complaints of this sort that rose on every side, I was glad that I was not President of the United States.

At the same time I DO think that the Government makes a mistake in taxing the profits of the poor book writers under the absurd name of INCOME. But let that go. The Kaiser would probably treat us worse.

I.--Some Startling Side Effects of the War

"There is no doubt," said Mr. Taft recently, "that the war is destined to effect the most profound uplift and changes, not only in our political outlook, but upon our culture, our thought and, most of all, upon our literature."

I am not absolutely certain that Mr. Taft really said this. He may not have said "uplift." But I seem to have heard something about uplift, somewhere. At any rate, there is no doubt of the fact that our literature has moved--up or down. Yes, the war is not only destined to affect our literature, but it has already done so. The change in outlook, in literary style, in mode of expression, even in the words themselves is already here.

Anybody can see it for himself by turning over the pages of our fashionable novels or by looking at the columns of our great American and English newspapers and periodicals.

But stop,--let me show what I mean by examples. I have them here in front of me. Take, for example, the London Spectator. Everybody recognised in it a model of literary dignity and decorum. Even those who read it least, admitted this most willingly; in fact, perhaps all the more so. In its pages to-day one finds an equal dignity of thought, yet, somehow, the wording seems to have undergone an alteration. One cannot say just where the change comes in. It is what the French call a je ne sais quoi, a something insaisissable, a sort of nuance, not amounting of course to a lueur, but still,--how shall one put it,--SOMETHING.

The example that is given below was taken almost word for word (indeed some of the words actually were so) from the very latest copy of The Spectator.

EDITORIAL FROM THE LONDON "SPECTATOR"

Showing the Stimulating Effect of the War on Its Literary Style

"There is no doubt that our boys, and the Americans, are going some on the western front. We have no hesitation in saying that last week's scrap was a cinch for the boys. It is credibly reported by our correspondent at The Hague that the German Emperor, the Crown Prince and a number of other guys were eye witnesses of the fight. If so, they got the surprise of their young lives. While we should not wish to show anything less than the chivalrous consideration for a beaten enemy which has been a tradition of our nation, we feel it is but just to say that for once the dirty pups got what was coming to them. We are glad to learn from official quarters that His Majesty King George has been graciously pleased to telegraph to General Pershing, 'Soak it to 'em--and THEN some.'

"Meantime the situation from the point of view both of terrain and of tactics remains altogether in our favour. The deep salient driven into the German lines near Soissons threatens to break up their communications and force a withdrawal on a wide front. We cannot make the position clearer to our English readers than by saying that our new lines occupy, as it were, the form of a baseball diamond, with Soissons at second base and with our headquarters at the home plate and our artillery support at third. Our readers will at once grasp the fact that, with our advance pivoted on the pitcher's box and with adequate cover at short, the thing is a lead-pipe cinch, --in fact, we have them lashed to the mast.

"Meantime the mood of the hour should be one, not of undue confidence or boastfulness, but of quiet resolution and deep thankfulness. As the Archbishop of Canterbury so feelingly put it in his sermon in Westminster Abbey last Sunday, 'Now that we have them by the neck let us go on, in deep and steadfast purpose, till we have twisted the gizzard out of them.'

"The Archbishop's noble words should, and will, re-echo in every English home."

Critical people may be inclined to doubt the propriety, or even the propinquity, of some of the literary changes due to the war. But there can be no doubt of the excellent effect of one of them, namely, the increasing knowledge and use among us of the pleasant language of France. It is no exaggeration to say that, before the war, few people in the United States, even among the colored population, spoke French with ease. In fact, in some cases the discomfort was so obvious as to be almost painful. This is now entirely altered. Thanks to our military guide-books, and to the general feeling of the day, our citizens are setting themselves to acquire the language of our gallant ally. And the signs are that they will do it. One hears every day in metropolitan society such remarks as, "Have you read, 'Soo le foo?'" "Oh, you mean that book by Haingri Barbooze? No, I have not read it yet, but I have read 'Mong Swassant Quinz' you know, by that other man."

This is hopeful indeed. Nor need we wonder that our best magazines are reflecting the same tendency.

Here for instance are the opening sentences of a very typical serial now running in one of our best periodicals: for all I know the rest of the sentences may be like them. At any rate, any magazine reader will recognize them at once:

BONNE MERE PITOU

A Conte of Old Normandy

Bonne Mere Pitou sat spinning beside the porte of the humble chaumiere in which she dwelt. From time to time her eyes looked up and down the gran' route that passed her door.

"Il ne vient pas," she murmured (he does not come).

She rose wearily and went dedans. Presently she came out again, dehors. "Il ne vient toujours pas," she sighed (he still does not come).

About her in the tall trees of the allee the percherons twittered while the soft roucoulement of the bees murmured drowsily in the tall calice of the chou-fleur.

"Il n'est pas venu," she said (perfect tense, third singular, he is not, or has not, come).

Can we blame him if he didn't? No doubt he was still studying his active verb before tackling Mere Pitou.

But there! Let it pass. In any case it is not only the magazines, but the novels themselves, that are being transformed by the war. Witness this:

BY ONE OF OUR MOST POPULAR NOVELISTS

"It was in the summer house, at the foot of the old garden, that the awaited declaration came. Edwin kneeled at Angelina's feet. At last they were alone! The successful barrage of conversation which he had put up at breakfast had compelled her mother to remain in her trenches, and had driven her father to the shelter of his dug-out. Her younger brother he had camouflaged with the present of a new fishing rod, thus inducing him to retire to the river. The communications with the servants had been cut. Of the strict neutrality of the gardener he was already assured. Edwin felt that the moment had come for going over the top. Yet being an able strategist, he was anxious not to attempt to advance on too wide a front.

"Angelina!" he exclaimed, raising himself to one knee with his hands outstretched toward her. The girl started as at the sound of an air bomb; for a moment she elevated her eyes and looked him full in the tangent, then she lowered them again but continued to observe him through her mental periscope.

"Angelina," he repeated, "I have a declaration to make."

"As from what date?" she questioned quietly. Edwin drew his watch from his pocket.

"As from this morning, at ten-forty-six," he said. Then, emboldened by her passive attitude, he continued with rising passion in his tone.

"Ever since I first met you I have felt that I could not live without you. I am a changed man. My calibre is altered. I feel ten centimeters wider in the mouth than I did six weeks ago. I feel that my path is altered. I have a new range and an angle of elevation such as I never experienced before. I have hidden my love as best I could till now. I have worn a moral gas-mask before your family. I can do so no longer. Angelina, will you be mine, forming with me a single unit, drawing our rations from the same field kitchen and occupying the same divisional headquarters?"

The girl seemed to hesitate. She raised her eyes to his.

"We know one another so little," she murmured.

Edwin felt that his offensive was failing. He therefore hastened to bring up his means of support.

"I have an ample income of my own," he pleaded.

Angelina raised her eyes again. It was evident that she was about to surrender. But at this moment her mother's voice was heard calling, "Angelina, Angelina, my dear, where are you?"

The barrage had broken down.

"Quick," said the girl, "mobilize yourself. Pick up that tennis racket and let us hurry to the court and dig ourselves in."

"But my declaration," urged Edwin eagerly.

"Accepted," she said, "as from eleven-two this morning."

V.--Other Impossibilities

1.--The Art of Conversation

I--HOW TO INTRODUCE TWO PEOPLE TO ONE ANOTHER

Nothing is more important in introducing two people to each other than to employ a fitting form of words. The more usually recognized forms are easily learned and committed to memory and may be utilized as occasion requires. I pass over such rudimentary formulas as "Ed, shake hands with Jim Taylor," or, "Boys, this is Pete, the new hand; Pete, get hold of the end of that cant-hook." In fact, we are speaking only of polite society as graced by the fair sex, the only kind that we need care about.

The Third Avenue Procedure

A very neat and convenient form is that in vogue in Third Avenue circles, New York, as, for instance, at a fifty-cents-a-head dance (ladies free) in the hall of the Royal Knights of Benevolence.

"Miss Summerside, meet Mr. O'Hara," after which Miss Summerside says very distinctly, "Mr. O'Hara," and Mr. O'Hara says with equal clearness "Miss Summerside." In this circle a mark of exquisite breeding is found in the request to have the name repeated. "I don't quite catch the name!" says Mr. O'Hara critically; then he catches it and repeats it--"Miss Summerside."

"Catching the name" is a necessary part of this social encounter. If not caught the first time it must be put over again. The peculiar merit of this introduction is that it lets Miss Summerside understand clearly that Mr. O'Hara never heard of her before. That helps to keep her in her place.

In superior circles, however, introduction becomes more elaborate, more flattering, more unctuous. It reaches its acme in what everyone recognizes at once as

The Clerical Method

This is what would be instinctively used in Anglican circles--as, for example, by the Episcopal Bishop of Boof in introducing a Canon of the Church to one of the "lady workers" of the congregation (meaning a lady too rich to work) who is expected to endow a crib in the Diocesan Home for Episcopal Cripples. A certain quantity of soul has to be infused into this introduction. Anybody who has ever heard it can fill in the proper accentuation, which must be very rich and deep.

"Oh, Mrs. Putitover, MAY I introduce my very dear old friend, Canon Cutitout? The Canon, Mrs. Putitover, is one of my DEAREST friends. Mrs. Putitover, my dear Canon, is quite one of our most enthusiastic workers."

After which outburst of soul the Bishop is able to add, "Will you excuse me, I'm afraid I simply MUST run."

Personally, I have never known or met a Bishop in society in any other situation than just about to run. Where they run to, I do not know. But I think I understand what they run from.

The Lounge Room of the Club

Equally high in the social scale but done quite differently is the Club Introduction. It is done by a club man who, for the life of him, can't remember the names of either of the two club men whom he is introducing, and who each, for the life of him, can't think of the name of the man they are being introduced by. It runs--

"Oh, I say, I beg your pardon--I thought, of course, you two fellows knew one another perfectly well--let me introduce--urr----wurr----"

Later on, after three whiskey-and-sodas, each of the three finds out the names of the other two, surreptitiously from the hall porter. But it makes no difference. They forget them again anyway. Now let us move up higher, in fact, very high. Let us approach the real thing.

Introduction to H.E. the Viceroy of India, K.C.B., K.C.S.I., S.O.S.

The most exalted form of introduction is seen in the presentation of Mr. Tomkins, American tourist, to H.E. the Viceroy of India. An aide-de-camp in uniform at the foot of a grand staircase shouts, "Mr. Tomkins!" An aide-de-camp at the top (one minute later) calls "Mr. Thompson"; another aide, four feet further on, calls "Mr. Torps."

Then a military secretary, standing close to His Excellency, takes Mr. Tomkins by the neck and bends him down toward the floor and says very clearly and distinctly, "Mr. Torpentine." Then he throws him out by the neck into the crowd beyond and calls for another. The thing is done. Mr. Tomkins wipes the perspiration from his hair with his handkerchief and goes back at full speed to the Hoogli Hotel, Calcutta, eager for stationery to write at once to Ohio and say that he knows the Viceroy.

The Office Introduction, One-sided

This introduction comes into our office, slipping past whoever keeps the door with a packet of books under its arm. It says--

"Ledd me introduze myself. The book proposition vidge I am introduzing is one vidge ve are now pudding on the market..."

Then, of two things, one--

Either a crash of glass is heard as the speaker is hurled through the skylight, or he walks out twenty minutes later, bowing profusely as he goes, and leaving us gazing in remorse at a signed document entitling us to receive the "Masterpieces of American Poetry" in sixty volumes.

On the Stage

Everything on the stage is done far better than in real life. This is true of introductions. There is a warmth, a soul, in the stage introduction not known in the chilly atmosphere of everyday society. Let me quote as an example of a stage introduction the formula used, in the best melodramatic art, in the kitchen-living-room (stove right centre) of the New England farm.

"Neighbour Jephson's son, this is my little gal, as good and sweet a little gal, as mindful of her old father, as you'll find in all New England. Neighbour Jephson's son, she's been my all in all to me, this little gal, since I laid her mother in the ground five Christmases ago--" The speaker is slightly overcome and leans against a cardboard clock for strength: he recovers and goes on--"Hope, this is Neighbour Jephson's son, new back from over the seas, as fine a lad, gal, if he's like the folk that went before him, as ever followed the sea. Hope, your hand. My boy, your hand. See to his comfort, Hope, while I go and read the Good Book a spell in the barnyard."

The Indian Formula

Many people, tired of the empty phrases of society, look back wistfully to the simple direct speech of savage life. Such persons will find useful the usual form of introduction (the shorter form) prevalent among our North American Indians (at least as gathered from the best literary model):

"Friends and comrades who are worthy,
See and look with all your eyesight,
Listen with your sense of hearing,
Gather with your apprehension--
Bow your heads, O trees, and hearken.
Hush thy rustling, corn, and listen;
Turn thine ear and give attention;
Ripples of the running water,
Pause a moment in your channels--
Here I bring you,--Hiawatha."

The last line of this can be changed to suit the particular case. It can just as easily read, at the end, "Here is Henry Edward Eastwood," or, "Here is Hal McGiverin, Junior," or anything else. All names fit the sense. That, in fact, was the wonderful art of Longfellow--the sense being independent of the words.

The Platform Introduction

Here is a form of introduction cruelly familiar to those who know it. It is used by the sour-looking villain facetiously called in newspaper reports the "genial chairman" of the meeting. While he is saying it the victim in his little chair on the platform is a target for the eyes of a thousand people who are wondering why he wears odd socks.

"The next speaker, ladies and gentlemen, is one who needs no introduction to this gathering. His name" (here the chairman consults a little card) "is one that has become a household word. His achievements in" (here the chairman looks at his card again, studies it, turns it upside down and adds) "in many directions are familiar to all of you." There is a feeble attempt at applause and the chairman then lifts his hand and says in a plain business-like tone--"Will those of the audience who are leaving kindly step as lightly as possible." He is about to sit down, but then adds as a pleasant afterthought for the speaker to brood over--"I may say, while I am on my feet, that next week our society is to have a REAL treat in hearing--et cetera and so forth--"

II--HOW TO OPEN A CONVERSATION

After the ceremony of introduction is completed the next thing to consider is the proper way to open a conversation. The beginning of conversation is really the hardest part. It is the social equivalent to "going over the top." It may best be studied in the setting and surroundings of the Evening Reception, where people stand upright and agonise, balancing a dish of ice-cream. Here conversation reaches its highest pitch of social importance. One must talk or die. Something may be done to stave it off a little by vigorous eating. But the food at such affairs is limited. There comes a point when it is absolutely necessary to say something.

The beginning, as I say, is the hardest problem. Other communities solve it better than we do.

The Chinese System

In China conversation, between strangers after introduction, is always opened by the question, "And how old are YOU?" This strikes me as singularly apt and sensible. Here is the one thing that is common ground between any two people, high or low, rich or poor--how far are you on your pilgrimage in life?

The Penetentiary Method

Compare with the Chinese method the grim, but very significant formula that is employed (I believe it is a literal fact) in the exercise yards of the American penitentiaries. "What have YOU brought?" asks the San Quentin or Sing Sing convict of the new arrival, meaning, "And how long is your sentence?" There is the same human touch about this, the same common ground of interest, as in the Chinese formula.

Polite Society

But in our polite society we have as yet found no better method than beginning with a sort of medical diagnosis--"How do you do?" This admits of no answer. Convention forbids us to reply in detail that we are feeling if anything slightly lower than last week, but that though our temperature has risen from ninety-one-fifty to ninety-one-seventy-five, our respiration is still normal.

Still worse is the weather as an opening topic. For it either begins and ends as abruptly as the medical diagnosis, or it leads the two talkers on into a long and miserable discussion of the weather of yesterday, of the day before yesterday, of last month, of last year and the last fifty years.

Let one beware, however, of a conversation that begins too easily.

The Mutual Friends' Opening

This can be seen at any evening reception, as when the hostess introduces two people who are supposed to have some special link to unite them at once with an instantaneous snap, as when, for instance, they both come from the same town.

"Let me introduce Mr. Sedley," said the hostess. "I think you and Mr. Sedley are from the same town, Miss Smiles. Miss Smiles, Mr. Sedley."

Off they go at a gallop. "I'm so delighted to meet you," says Mr. Sedley. "It's good to hear from anybody who comes from our little town." (If he's a rollicking humourist, Mr. Sedley calls it his little old "burg.")

"Oh, yes," answers Miss Smiles. "I'm from Winnipeg too. I was so anxious to meet you to ask if you knew the McGowans. They're my greatest friends at home."

"The--who?" asks Mr. Sedley.

"The McGowans--on Selkirk Avenue."

"No-o, I don't think I do. I know the Prices on Selkirk Avenue. Of course you know them."

"The Prices? No, I don't believe I do--I don't think I ever heard of the Prices. You don't mean the Pearsons? I know them very well."

"No, I don't know the Pearsons. The Prices live just near the reservoir."

"No, then I'm sure I don't know them. The Pearsons live close to the college."

"Close to the College? Is it near the William Kennedys?"

"I don't think I know the William Kennedys."

This is the way the conversation goes on for ten minutes. Both Mr. Sedley and

Miss Smiles are getting desperate. Their faces are fixed. Their sentences are reduced to--

"Do you know the Petersons?"

"No. Do you know the Appleby's?"

"No. Do you know the Willie Johnsons?"

"No."

Then at last comes a rift in the clouds. One of them happens to mention Beverley Dixon. The other is able to cry exultingly--

"Beverley Dixon? Oh, yes, rather. At least, I don't KNOW him, but I used often to hear the Applebys speak of him."

And the other exclaims with equal delight--

"I don't know him very well either, but I used to hear the Willie Johnsons talk about him all the time."

They are saved.

Half an hour after they are still standing there talking of Beverly Dixon.

The Etiquette Book

Personally I have suffered so much from inability to begin a conversation that not long ago I took the extreme step of buying a book on the subject. I regret to say that I got but little light or help from it. It was written by the Comtesse de Z--. According to the preface the Comtesse had "moved in the highest circles of all the European capitals." If so, let her go on moving there. I for one, after trying her book, shall never stop her. This is how the Comtesse solves the problem of opening a conversation:

"In commencing a conversation, the greatest care should be devoted to the selection of a topic, good taste demanding that one should sedulously avoid any subject of which one's vis-a-vis may be in ignorance. Nor are the mere words alone to be considered. In the art of conversation much depends upon manner. The true conversationalist must, in opening, invest himself with an atmosphere of interest and solicitude. He must, as we say in French, be prepared to payer les rais de la conversation. In short, he must 'give himself an air.'"

There! Go and do it if you can. I admit that I can't. I have no idea what the French phrase above means, but I know that personally I cannot "invest myself with an atmosphere of interest." I might manage about two per cent on five hundred dollars. But what is that in these days of plutocracy?

At any rate I tried the Comtesse's directions at a reception last week, on being introduced to an unknown lady. And they failed. I cut out nearly all the last part, and confined myself merely to the proposed selection of a topic, endeavouring to pick it with as much care as if I were selecting a golf club out of a bag. Naturally I had to confine myself to the few topics that I know about, and on which I can be quite interesting if I get started.

"Do you know any mathematics?" I asked.

"No," said the lady.

This was too bad. I could have shown her some good puzzles about the squares of the prime numbers up to forty-one.

I paused and gave myself more air.

"How are you," I asked, "on hydrostatics?"

"I beg your pardon," she said. Evidently she was ignorant again.

"Have you ever studied the principles of aerial navigation?" I asked.

"No," She answered.

I was pausing again and trying to invest myself with an air of further interest, when another man was introduced to her, quite evidently, from his appearance, a vapid jackass without one tenth of the brain calibre that I have.

"Oh, how do you do?" he said. "I say, I've just heard that Harvard beat Princeton this afternoon. Great, isn't it?"

In two minutes they were talking like old friends. How do these silly asses do it?

When Dressed Hogs are Dull

An equally unsuccessful type of conversation, often overheard at receptions, is where one of the two parties to it is too surly, too stupid, or too self-important and too rich to talk, and the other labours in vain.

The surly one is, let us say, a middle-aged, thick-set man of the type that anybody recognizes under the name Money Hog. This kind of person, as viewed standing in his dress suit, mannerless and stupid, too rich to have to talk and too dull to know how to, always recalls to my mind the head-line of the market reports in the newspapers, "Dressed Hogs are Dull."

The other party to the conversation is a winsome and agreeable woman, trying her best to do her social duty.

But, tenez, as the Comtesse of Z---- would say, I can exactly illustrate the position and attitude of the two of them from a recollection of my childhood. I remember that in one of my nursery books of forty years ago there was a picture entitled "The Lady in Love With A Swine." A willowy lady in a shimmering gown leaned over the rail of a tessellated pig-sty, in which an impossibly clean hog stood in an attitude of ill-mannered immobility. With the picture was the rhyming legend,

There was a Lady in love with a swine,
"Honey," said she, "will you be mine?
I'll build you a silver sty
And in it you shall lie."
"Honk!" said He.

There was something, as I recall it, in the sweet willingness of the Lady that was singularly appealing, and contrasted with the dull mannerless passivity of the swine.

In each of the little stanzas that followed, the pretty advances of the Lady were rebuffed by a surly and monosyllabic "honk" from the hog.

Here is the social counterpart of the scene in the picture-book. Mr. Grunt, capitalist, is standing in his tessellated sty,--the tessellated sty being represented by the hardwood floor of a fashionable drawing-room. His face is just the same as the face of the pig in the picture-book. The willowy lady, in the same shimmering clothes and with the same pretty expression of eagerness, is beside him.

"Oh, Mr. Grunt," she is saying, "how interesting it must be to be in your place and feel such tremendous power. Our hostess was just telling me that you own practically all the shoemaking machinery factories--it IS shoe-making machinery, isn't it?--east of Pennsylvania."

"Honk!" says Mr. Grunt.

"Shoe-making machinery," goes on the willowy lady (she really knows nothing and cares less about it) "must be absolutely fascinating, is it not?"

"Honk!" says Mr. Grunt.

"But still you must find it sometimes a dreadful strain, do you not? I mean, so much brain work, and that sort of thing."

"Honk!" says Mr. Grunt.

"I should love so much to see one of your factories. They must be so interesting."

"Honk!" says Mr. Grunt. Then he turns and moves away sideways. Into his little piggy eyes has come a fear that the lady is going to ask him to subscribe to something, or wants a block of his common stock, or his name on a board of directors. So he leaves her. Yet if he had known it she is probably as rich as he is, or richer, and hasn't the faintest interest in his factories, and never intends to go near one. Only she is fit to move and converse in polite society and Mr. Grunt is not.

2.--Heroes and Heroines

"What are you reading?" I asked the other day of a blue-eyed boy of ten curled up among the sofa cushions.

He held out the book for me to see.

"Dauntless Ned among the Cannibals," he answered.

"Is it exciting?" I enquired.

"Not very," said the child in a matter-of-fact tone. "But it's not bad."

I took the book from him and read aloud at the opened page.

"In a compact mass the gigantic savages rushed upon our hero, shrieking with rage and brandishing their huge clubs. Ned stood his ground fearlessly, his back to a banana tree. With a sweep of his cutlass he severed the head of the leading savage from his body, while with a back stroke of his dirk he stabbed another to the heart. But resistance against such odds was vain. By sheer weight of numbers, Ned was borne to the ground. His arms were then pinioned with stout ropes made of the fibres of the boobooda tree. With shrieks of exultation the savages dragged our hero to an opening in the woods where a huge fire was burning, over which was suspended an enormous caldron of bubbling oil. 'Boil him, boil him,' yelled the savages, now wrought to the point of frenzy."

"That seems fairly exciting, isn't it?" I said.

"Oh, he won't get boiled," said the little boy. "He's the hero."

So I knew that the child has already taken his first steps in the disillusionment of fiction.

Of course he was quite right as to Ned. This wonderful youth, the hero with whom we all begin an acquaintance with books, passes unhurt through a thousand perils. Cannibals, Apache Indians, war, battles, shipwrecks, leave him quite unscathed. At the most Ned gets a flesh wound which is healed, in exactly one paragraph, by that wonderful drug called a "simple."

But the most amazing thing about this particular hero, the boy Ned, is the way in which he turns up in all the great battles and leading events of the world.

It was Ned, for example, who at the critical moment at Gettysburg turned in his saddle to General Meade and said quietly, "General, the day is ours." "If it is," answered Meade, as he folded his field glass, "you alone, Ned, have saved it."

In the same way Ned was present at the crossing of the Delaware with Washington. Thus:--

"'What do you see, Ned?' said Washington, as they peered from the leading boat into the driving snow.

"'Ice,' said Ned. 'My boy,' said the Great American General, and a tear froze upon his face as he spoke, 'you have saved us all.'"

Here is Ned at Runningmede when King John with his pen in hand was about to sign the Magna Carta.

"For a moment the King paused irresolute, the uplifted quill in his hand, while his crafty, furtive eyes indicated that he might yet break his plighted faith with the assembled barons.

"Ned laid his mailed hand upon the parchment.

"'Sign it,' he said sternly, 'or take the consequences.'

"The King signed.

"'Ned,' said the Baron de Bohun, as he removed his iron vizor from his bronze face, 'thou hast this day saved all England.'"

In the stories of our boyhood in which Ned figured, there was no such thing as a heroine, or practically none. At best she was brought in as an afterthought. It was announced on page three hundred and one that at the close of Ned's desperate adventures in the West Indies he married the beautiful daughter of Don Diego, the Spanish governor of Portobello; or else, at the end of the great war with Napoleon, that he married a beautiful and accomplished French girl whose parents had perished in the Revolution.

Ned generally married away from home. In fact his marriages were intended to cement the nations, torn asunder by Ned's military career. But sometimes he returned to his native town, all sunburned, scarred and bronzed from battle (the bronzing effect of being in battle is always noted): he had changed from a boy to a man: that is, from a boy of fifteen to a man of sixteen. In such a case Ned marries in his own home town. It is done after this fashion:

"But who is this who advances smiling to greet him as he crosses the familiar threshold of the dear old house? Can this tall, beautiful girl be Gwendoline, the child-playmate of his boyhood?"

Well, can it? I ask it of every experienced reader--can it or can it not?

Ned had his day, in the boyhood of each of us. We presently passed him by. I am speaking, of course, of those of us who are of maturer years and can look back upon thirty or forty years of fiction reading. "Ned," flourishes still, I understand, among the children of today. But now he flies in aeroplanes, and dives in submarines, and gives his invaluable military advice to General Joffre and General Pershing.

But with the oncoming of adolescent years something softer was needed than Ned with his howling cannibals and his fusillade of revolver shots.

So the "Ned" of the Adventure Books was supplanted by the Romantic Heroine of the Victorian Age and the Long-winded Immaculate who accompanied her as the Hero.

I do not know when these two first opened their twin career. Whether Fenimore Cooper or Walter Scott began them, I cannot say. But they had an undisputed run on two continents for half a century.

This Heroine was a sylph. Her chiefest charm lay in her physical feebleness. She was generally presented to us in some such words as these:

"Let us now introduce to our readers the fair Madeline of Rokewood. Slender and graceful and of a form so fragile that her frame scarce fitted to fulfil its bodily functions...she appeared rather as one of those ethereal beings of the air who might visit for a brief moment this terrestrial scene, than one of its earthly inhabitants. Her large, wondering eyes looked upon the beholder in childlike innocence."

Sounds simple, doesn't it? One might suspect there was something wrong with the girl's brain. But listen to this:--

"The mind of Madeline, elegantly formed by the devoted labours of the venerable Abbe, her tutor, was of a degree of culture rarely found in one so young. Though scarce eighteen summers had flown over her head at the time when we introduce her to our readers, she was intimately conversant with the French, Italian, Spanish, and Provencal tongues. The abundant pages of history, both ancient and modern, sacred and profane, had been opened for her by her devoted instructor. In music she played with exquisite grace and accuracy upon both the spinet and the harpsichord, while her voice, though lacking something in compass, was sweet and melodious to a degree."

From such a list of accomplishments it is clear that Madeline could have matriculated, even at the Harvard Law School, with five minutes preparation. Is it any wonder that there was a wild rush for Madeline? In fact, right after the opening description of the Heroine, there follows an ominous sentence such as this:--

"It was this exquisite being whose person Lord Rip de Viperous, a man whose reputation had shamed even the most licentious court of the age, and had led to his banishment from the presence of the king, had sworn to get within his power."

Personally I don't blame Lord Rip a particle; it must have been very rough on him to have been banished from the presence of the king--enough to inflame a man to do anything.

With two such characters in the story, the scene was set and the plot and adventures followed as a matter of course. Lord Rip de Viperous pursued the Heroine. But at every step he is frustrated. He decoys Madeline to a ruined tower at midnight, her innocence being such and the gaps left in her education by the Abbe being so wide, that she is unaware of the danger of ruined towers after ten thirty P.M. In fact, "tempted by the exquisite clarity and fulness of the moon, which magnificent orb at this season spread its widest effulgence over all nature, she accepts the invitation of her would-be-betrayer to gather upon the battlements of the ruined keep the strawberries which grew there in wild profusion."

But at the critical moment, Lord de Viperous is balked. At the very instant when he is about to seize her in his arms, Madeline turns upon him and says in such icy tones, "Titled villain that you are, unhand me," that the man is "cowed." He slinks down the ruined stairway "cowed." And at every later turn, at each renewed attempt, Madeline "cows" him in like fashion.

Moreover while Lord de Viperous is being thus cowed by Madeline the Heroine, he is also being "dogged" by the Hero. This counterpart of Madeline who shared
her popularity for fifty years can best be described as the Long-winded Immaculate
Hero. Entirely blameless in his morals, and utterly virtuous in his conduct, he pos-
sessed at least one means of defending himself. He could make speeches. This he
did on all occasions. With these speeches he "dogged" Lord de Viperous. Here is the
style of them:--

"'My Lord,' said Markham..." (incidentally let it be explained that this particular brand of hero was always known by his surname and his surname was always
Markham) --"'My lord, the sentiments that you express and the demeanour which
you have evinced are so greatly at variance with the title that you bear and the lin-
eage of which you spring that no authority that you can exercise and no threats that
you are able to command shall deter me from expressing that for which, however
poor and inadequate my powers of speech, all these of whom and for what I am
what I am, shall answer to it for the integrity of that, which, whether or not, is at
least as it is. My lord, I have done. Or shall I speak more plainly still?'"

Is it to be wondered that after this harangue Lord Rip sank into a chair, a hid-
eous convulsion upon his face, murmuring--"It is enough."

But successful as they were as Hero and Heroine, Markham and Madeline presently passed off the scene. Where they went to, I do not know. Perhaps Markham
got elected in the legislature of Massachusetts. At any rate they disappeared from
fiction.

There followed in place of Madeline, the athletic sunburned heroine with
the tennis racket. She was generally called Kate Middleton, or some such plain,
straightforward designation. She wore strong walking boots and leather leggings.
She ate beef steak. She shot with a rifle. For a while this Boots and Beef Heroine (of
the middle nineties) made a tremendous hit. She climbed crags in the Rockies. She
threw steers in Colorado with a lariat. She came out strong in sea scenes and shipwrecks, and on sinking steamers, where she "cowed" the trembling stewards and
"dogged" the mutinous sailors in the same fashion that Madeline used to "cow" and
"dog" Lord Rip de Viperous.

With the Boots and Beef Heroine went as her running mate the out-of-doors man, whose face had been tanned and whose muscles had been hardened into tempered steel in wild rides over the Pampas of Patagonia, and who had learned every art and craft of savage life by living among the wild Hoodoos of the Himalayas. This Air-and-Grass-man, as he may be called, is generally supposed to write the story... He was "I" all through. And he had an irritating modesty in speaking of his own prowess. Instead of saying straight out that he was the strongest and bravest man in the world, he implied it indirectly on every page.

Here, for example, is a typical scene in which "I" and Kate figure in a desperate adventure in the Rocky Mountains, pursued by Indians.

"We are about to descend on a single cord from the summit of a lofty crag, our sole chance of escape (and a frightfully small chance at that) from the roving band of Apaches.

"With my eye I measured the fearsome descent below us.

"'Hold fast to the line, Miss Middleton,' I said as I set my foot against a projecting rock. (Please note that the Air-and-Grass Hero in these stories always calls the Heroine Miss Middleton right up to the very end.)

"The noble girl seized the knotted end of the buckskin line. 'All right, Mr. Smith,' she said with quiet confidence.

"I braced myself for the effort. My muscles like tempered steel responded to the strain. I lowered a hundred fathoms of the line. I could already hear the voice of Kate far down the cliff.

"Don't let go the line, Miss Middleton,' I called. (Here was an excellent piece of advice.)

"The girl's clear voice floated up to me... 'All right, Mr. Smith,' she called, 'I won't.'"

Of course they landed safely at the foot of the cliff, after the manner of all heroes and heroines. And here it is that Kate in her turn comes out strong, at the evening encampment, frying bacon over a blazing fire of pine branches, while the firelight illuminates her leather leggings and her rough but picturesque costume.

The circumstances might seem a little daring and improper. But the reader knows that it is all right, because the hero and heroine always call one another Miss Middleton and Mr. Smith.

Not till right at the end, when they are just getting back again to the confines of civilization, do they depart from this.

Here is the scene that happens... The hero and heroine are on the platform of the way-side depot where they are to part... Kate to return to the luxurious home of her aunt, Mrs. van der Kyper of New York, and the Air-and-Grass Man to start for the pampas of Patagonia to hunt the hoopoo. The Air-and-Grass Man is about to say goodbye. Then... "'Kate,' I said, as I held the noble girl's gloved hand in mine a moment. She looked me in the face with the full, frank, fearless gaze of a sister.

"'Yes?' she answered.

"'Kate,' I repeated, 'do you know what I was thinking of when I held the line while you were half way down the cliff?'

"'No,' she murmured, while a flush suffused her cheek.

"'I was thinking, Kate,' I said, 'that if the rope broke I should be very sorry.'

"'Edward!' she exclaimed.

"I clasped her in my arms.

"'Shall I make a confession,' said Kate, looking up timidly, half an hour later, as I tenderly unclasped the noble girl from my encircling arms, ...'I was thinking the same thing too.'"

So Kate and Edward had their day and then, as Tennyson says, they "passed," or as less cultivated people put it, "they were passed up in the air."

As the years went by they failed to please. Kate was a great improvement upon Madeline. But she wouldn't do. The truth was, if one may state it openly, Kate wasn't TOUGH enough. In fact she wasn't tough at all. She turned out to be in reality just as proper and just as virtuous as Madeline.

So, too, with the Air-and-Grass Hero. For all of his tempered muscles and his lariat and his Winchester rifle, he was presently exposed as a fraud. He was just as Long-winded and just as Immaculate as the Victorian Hero that he displaced.

What the public really wants and has always wanted in its books is wickedness. Fiction was recognised in its infancy as being a work of the devil.

So the popular novel, despairing of real wickedness among the cannibals, and in the ruined tower at midnight, and on the open-air of the prairies, shifted its scenes again. It came indoors. It came back to the city. And it gave us the new crop of heroes and heroines and the scenes and settings with which the fiction of to-day has replaced the Heroes and Heroines of Yesterday. The Lure of the City is its theme. It pursues its course to the music of the ukalele, in the strident racket of the midnight cabaret. Here move the Harvard graduate in his dinner jacket, drunk at one in the morning. Here is the hard face of Big Business scowling at its desk; and here the glittering Heroine of the hour in her dress of shimmering sequins, making such tepid creatures as Madeline and Kate look like the small change out of a twenty-five cent shinplaster.

3.--The Discovery of America;

Being Done into Moving Pictures and Out Again

"No greater power for education," said President Shurman the other day, "has come among us during the last forty years than the moving picture."

I am not certain that it was President Shurman. And he may not have said it the other day. Nor do I feel absolutely sure that he referred to the LAST forty years. Indeed now that I come to think of it, I don't believe it WAS Shurman. In fact it may have been ex-President Eliot. Or was it, perhaps, President Hadley of Yale? Or did I say it myself? Judging by the accuracy and force of the language, I think I must have. I doubt if Shurman or Hadley could have put it quite so neatly. There's a touch about it that I recognise.

But let that pass. At any rate it is something that everybody is saying and thinking. All our educators have turned their brains towards the possibility of utilising moving pictures for the purpose of education. It is being freely said that history and geography, and even arithmetic, instead of being taught by the slow and painful process of books and memory, can be imparted through the eye.

I had no sooner heard of this idea than I became impassioned to put it into practice. I have therefore prepared, or am preparing, a film, especially designed for the elementary classes of our schools to narrate the story of the discovery of America.

This I should like the reader to sit and see with me, in the eye of his imagination. But let me first give the plain, unvarnished account of the discovery of America as I took it from one of our school histories.

"Christopher Columbus, otherwise Christoforo Colombo,
the celebrated discoverer of America, was born of poor
but honest parents in the Italian city of Genoa. His
mother, Teresa Colombo, seems to have been a woman of
great piety and intelligence. Of his father, Bartolomeo
Colombo, nothing is recorded. From his earliest youth
the boy Christopher developed a passion for mathematics,
astronomy, geodesy, and the other sciences of the
day..."

But, no,--stop! I am going too fast. The reader will get it better if we turn it into pictures bit by bit as we go on. Let the reader therefore imagine himself seated before the curtain in the lighted theatre. All ready? Very good. Let the music begin--Star Spangled Banner, please--flip off the lights. Now then.

DISCOVERY OF AMERICA AUTHORIZED BY THE BOARD OF CENSORS OF NEW YORK STATE

There we are. That gives the child the correct historical background right away. Now what goes on next? Let me see. Ah, yes, of course. We throw an announcement on the screen, thus.

CHRISTOPHER COLUMBUS.. Mr. Quinn

Here the face of Mr. Quinn (in a bowler hat) is thrown on the screen and fades out again.

We follow him up with

SPIRIT OF AMERICA.. Miss E. Dickenson

Now, we are ready to begin in earnest. Let us make the scenario together. First idea to be expressed:

"Christopher Columbus was the son of poor but honest parents."

This might seem difficult to a beginner, but to those of us who frequent the movies it is nothing. The reel spins and we see--a narrow room--(it is always narrow in the movies)--to indicate straitened circumstances--cardboard furniture--high chairs with carved backs--two cardboard beams across the ceiling (all this means the Middle Ages)--a long dinner table--all the little Columbuses seated at it--Teresa Colombo cutting bread at one end of it--gives a slice to each, one slice (that means poverty in the movies)--Teresa rolls her eyes up--all the little children put their hands together and say grace (this registers honesty). The thing is done. Let us turn back to the history book and see what is to be put in next.

"...The father of Christopher, Bartolomeo Colombo, was a man of no especial talent of whom nothing is recorded."

That's easy. First we announce him on the screen:

BARTOLOMEO COLOMBO.. Mr. Henderson

Then we stick him on the film on a corner of the room, leaning up against the cardboard clock and looking at the children. This attitude in the movies always indicates a secondary character of no importance. His business is to look at the others and to indicate forgetfulness of self, incompetence, unimportance, vacuity, simplicity. Note how this differs from the attitudes of important characters. If a movie character--one of importance--is plotting or scheming, he seats himself at a little round table, drums on it with his fingers, and half closes one eye. If he is being talked to, or having a letter or document or telegram read to him, he stands "facing full" and working his features up and down to indicate emotion sweeping over them. If he is being "exposed" (which is done by pointing fingers at him), he hunches up like a snake in an angle of the room with both eyes half shut and his mouth set as if he had just eaten a lemon. But if he has none of these things to express and is only in the scene as a background for the others, then he goes over and leans in an easy attitude against the tall cardboard clock.

That then is the place for Bartolomeo Colombo. To the clock with him.

Now what comes next?

"...The young Christopher developed at an early age a passion for study, and especially for astronomy, geometry, geodesy, and the exact science of the day."

Quite easy. On spins the film. Young Christopher in a garret room (all movie study is done in garrets). The cardboard ceiling slopes within six inches of his head. This shows that the boy never rises from his books. He can't. On a table in front of him is a little globe and a pair of compasses. Christopher spins the globe round. Then he makes two circles with the compasses, one after the other, very carefully. This is the recognised movie symbol for mathematical research.

So there we have Christopher--poor, honest, studious, full of circles.

Now to the book again.

"...The young Columbus received his education at the monastery of the Franciscan monks at Genoa. Here he spent seven years."

Yes, but we can put that on the screen in seven seconds.

Turn on the film.

Movie Monastery--exterior, done in grey cardboard--ding, dong, ding, dong (man in the orchestra with triangle and stick)--procession of movie friars--faces more like thugs, but never mind--they are friars because they walk two and two in a procession, singing out of hymn books.

Now for the book again.

"...Fra Giacomo, the prior of the monastery, delighted with the boy's progress, encourages his studies."

Wait a minute.

FRA GIACOMO... Mr. Edward Sims

Mr. Sims's face, clean-shaved under a round hat fades in and out. Then the picture goes on. Movie monastery interior--young Christopher, still at a table with compasses--benevolent friar bending over him--Christopher turns the compasses and looks up with a what-do-you-know-about-that look--astonishment and delight of friar (registered by opening his eyes like a bull frog). All this shows study, progress, application. The friars are delighted with the boy.

"...Christopher, after seven years of study, reaches the firm conviction that the world is round."

Picture. Christopher--with his globe--jumps up from table--passes his fingers round and round the globe--registers the joy of invention--seats himself at table and draws circles with his compasses furiously. He fades out.

"...Fired with his discovery Christopher sets out from the monastery."

Stop a minute, this is a little hard. Fired. How can we show Christopher "fired." We can't. Perhaps he'll be fired if the film is no good, but we must omit it just now.

"He sets out."

One second only for this. Monastery door (double cardboard with iron across it)--Christopher leaving--carries a wallet to mean distance. Fra Giacomo blessing him--fade out.

"...For eighteen years Columbus vainly travelled through the world on foot offering his discovery at the courts of Europe, in vain, though asking nothing in return for it except a fleet of ships, two hundred men and provisions for two years."

To anybody not used to scenarios this looks a large order. Eighteen years seems difficult to put on the screen. In reality this is exactly where the trained movie man sees his chance. Here he can put in anything and everything that he likes, bringing in, in a slightly mediaeval form, all his favourite movie scenes.

Thus, for example, here we have first the good old midnight cabaret supper scene--thinly disguised as the court of the King of Sardinia. To turn a cabaret into a court the movie men merely exchange their Fifth Avenue evening dress for short coats and knee breeches, heavily wadded and quilted, and wear large wigs. Quilted pants and wigs register courtiers, the courtiers of anybody--Charlemagne, Queen Elizabeth, Peter the Great, Louis Quatorze, anybody and everybody who ever had courtiers. Just as men with bare legs mean Romans, men in pea-jackets mean detectives, and young men drunk in evening dress Harvard graduates.

The ladies at the court of Sardinia wear huge paper frills round their necks. Otherwise it is the cabaret scene with the familiar little tables, and the ukaleles going like mad in one corner, and black sarsaparilla being poured foaming into the glasses.

In this scene Columbus moves up and down, twirling his little globe and looking appealingly in their faces. All laugh at him. His part is just the same as that of the poor little girl trying to sell up-state violets in the midnight cabaret.

The Court of Sardinia fades and the film shows Columbus vainly soliciting financial aid from Lorenzo the Magnificent.

Stop one minute, please.

LORENZO THE MAGNIFICENT... Mr. L. Evans

This scene again is old and familiar. It is the well-known interior representing the Grinding Capitalist, or the Bitter Banker refusing aid to the boy genius who has invented a patent pea-rake. The only change is that Lorenzo wears a huge wig, has no telephone, and handles a large quill pen (to register Middle Ages) which he wiggles furiously up and down on a piece of parchment.

So the eighteen years, with scenes of this sort turn out the easiest part of the whole show.

But let us to the book again.

"...After eighteen years Columbus, now past the prime of life, is presented at the Court of Queen Isabella of Spain."

Just half a moment.

QUEEN ISABELLA.. Miss Janet Briggs

There will be very probably at this point a slight applause from the back of the hall. Miss Briggs was here last week, or her astral body was--as Maggie of the Cattle Ranges. The impression that she made is passed on to Isabella.

"The Queen and her consort, King Ferdinand of Aragon..."

Stop, stick him on the film.

FERDINAND OF ARAGON.. Mr. Edward Giles

(Large wig, flat velvet cap and square whiskers--same make-up as for Ferdinand of Bulgaria, Ferdinand of Bohemia, or any of the Ferdinands.)

"...were immediately seized with enthusiasm for the marvellous discovery of the Genoese adventurer."

Picture. Columbus hands his globe to Isabella and his compasses to Ferdinand. They register delight and astonishment. The Queen turns the globe round and round and holds it up to Ferdinand. Both indicate with their faces, well-what-do-you-know-about-this. Ferdinand makes a circle with the compasses on a table--the courtiers, fickle creatures, crowd around. They are still dressed as in Sardinia eighteen years ago. In fact, one recognises quite a lot of them. When Ferdinand draws the circle they fall back in wild astonishment, gesticulating frantically. What they mean is, "It's a circle, it's a circle."

"The King and Queen at once place three ships at the disposal of Columbus."

On with the picture. The harbour of the port of Palos-- ships bobbing up and down (it is really the oyster boats in Baltimore Bay but it looks just like Palos, or near enough). Notice Queen Isabella on the right, at the top of a flight of steps, extending her hand and looking at Columbus. Her gesture means, "Pick a ship, any ship you like, any colour." Just as if she were saying, "Pick a card, any card you like."

We turn again to the history.

"...Christopher Columbus, now arrived at the height of his desire, sets out upon his memorable voyage accompanied by a hundred companions in three caravels, the Pinta, the Nina and the Espiritu Santo."

Ah, here we have the movie work--the real thing. Cardboard caravel tossing on black water--seen first right close to us--we are almost on board of it. Notice the movie sailors with black whiskers and bare feet (bare feet in the movies always means a sailor, and black whiskers mean Spaniards). Now we see the caravel a little way out--whoop! How she bobs up and down! They give her that jolt (it's done with the machine itself) to mean danger. There are all three caravels--Hoop--er--oo! See them go up and down--stormy night coming all right. See the sun setting in the west, over the water? They're heading straight for it. Good-night Columbus--take care of yourself out there in the blackness.

"During the voyage Columbus remained continually on deck. Sleeping at the prow, his face towards the new world, he saw already in his dreams the accomplishment of his hopes."

On goes the picture. Christopher in the prow of the caravel (in the movies a prow is made by putting two little board fences together and propping up a bowsprit lengthwise over them). Columbus sits up, peers intently into the darkness, his hand to his brow--registers a look. Do I see America? No. Lies down, shuts his eyes and falls into an instantaneous movie sleep. His face fades out slowly to music, which means that he is going to dream. Then on the screen the announcement is shown:

SPIRIT OF AMERICA... Miss E. Dickenson

and here we have Miss Dickenson floating in the air above Columbus. She wears nothing except mosquito netting, but she has got on enough of it to get past the censor of the State of New York. Just enough, apparently.

Miss E. Dickenson is joined by a whole troop of Miss Dickensons all in white mosquito netting. They go through a series of beautiful evolutions, floating over the sleeping figure of Columbus. The dance they do is meant to typify, or rather to signify,--as a matter of fact we needn't worry much about what it signified. It is an allegory, done in white mosquito netting. That is generally held to be quite enough. Let us go back to the book--

"After a storm-tossed voyage of three months..."

Wait a bit. Turn on the picture again and toss the caravels up and down.

"...during which the food supply threatened to fail..."

Put that on the screen, please. Columbus surrounded by ten sailors, dividing up a potato.

"...the caravels arrived in safety at the beautiful island of San Salvador. Columbus, bearing the banner of Spain, stepped first ashore. Surrounded by a wondering crowd of savages he prostrated himself upon the beach and kissed the soil of the New World that he had discovered."

All this is so easy that it's too easy. It runs into pictures of itself. Anybody, accustomed to the movies, can see Columbus with his banner and the movie savages hopping up and down around him. Movie savages are gay, gladsome creatures anyway, and hopping up and down is their chief mode of expressing themselves. Add to them a sandy beach, with palm trees waving visibly in the wind (it is always windy in the movies) and the thing is done.

Just one further picture is needed to complete the film.

"Columbus who returned to Europe to lay at the feet of the Spanish sovereigns the world he had discovered, fell presently under the disfavour of the court, and died in poverty and obscurity, a victim of the ingratitude of princes."

Last picture. Columbus dying under the poignant circumstances known only in the movies--a garret room--ceiling lower than ever--a truckle bed, narrow enough to kill him if all else failed--Teresa Colombo his aged mother alone at his bedside--she offers him medicine in a long spoon--(this shows, if nothing else would, that the man is ill)--he shakes his head--puts out his hand and rests it on the little globe--reaches feebly for his compasses--can't manage it--rolls up his eyes and fades.

The music plays softly and the inexorable film, like the reel of life itself, spins on, announcing

At this theatre
All next week

MAGGIE MAY
and
WALTER CURRAN
in
IS IT WORTH IT

And after that I can imagine the audience dispersing, and the now educated children going off to their homes and one saying as he enters--

"Gee, I seen a great picture show at school to-day."

"Yes?" says his mother, "and what was it?"

"Oh, it was all about a gink that went round the cabarets trying to sell an invention what he'd got but nobody wouldn't look at it till at last one dame gave him three oyster boats, see? and so he and a lot of other guys loaded them up and hiked off across the ocean."

"And where did he go to?"

"Africa. And he and the other guys had a great stand in with the natives and he'd have sold his invention all right but one old dame got him alone in a hut and poisoned him and took it off him."

That, I think, is about the way the film would run. When it is finished I must get President Shurman, or whoever it was, to come and see it.

4.--Politics from Within

To avoid all error as to the point of view, let me say in commencing that I am a Liberal Conservative, or, if you will, a Conservative Liberal with a strong dash of sympathy with the Socialist idea, a friend of Labour, and a believer in Progressive Radicalism. I do not desire office but would take a seat in the Canadian Senate at five minutes notice.

I believe there are ever so many people of exactly this way of thinking.

Let me say further than in writing of "politics" I am only dealing with the lights and shadows that flicker over the surface, and am not trying to discuss, still less to decry, the deep and vital issues that lie below.

Yet I will say that vital though the issues may be below the surface, there is more clap-trap, insincerity and humbug on the surface of politics than over any equal area on the face of any institution.

The candidate, as such, is a humbug. The voters, as voters--not as fathers, brothers or sons--are humbugs. The committees are humbugs. And the speeches to the extent of about ninety per cent are pure buncombe. But, oddly enough, out of the silly babel of talk that accompanies popular government, we get, after all, pretty good government--infinitely better than the government of an autocratic king. Between democracy and despotic kingship lies all the difference between genial humbug and black sin.

For the candidate for popular office I have nothing but sympathy and sorrow. It has been my fortune to walk round at the heels of half a dozen of them in different little Canadian towns, watching the candidate try in vain to brighten up his face at the glad sight of a party voter.

One, in particular, I remember. Nature had meant him to be a sour man, a hard man, a man with but little joy in the company of his fellows. Fate had made him a candidate for the House of Commons. So he was doing his best to belie his nature.

"Hullo, William!" he would call out as a man passed driving a horse and buggy, "got the little sorrel out for a spin, eh?"

Then he would turn to me and say in a low rasping voice--

"There goes about the biggest skunk in this whole constituency."

A few minutes later he would wave his hand over a little hedge in friendly salutation to a man working in a garden.

"Hullo, Jasper! That's a fine lot of corn you've got there."

Jasper replied in a growl. And when we were well past the house the candidate would say between his teeth--

"That's about the meanest whelp in the riding."

Our conversation all down the street was of that pattern.

"Good morning, Edward! Giving the potatoes a dose of Paris green, eh?"

And in an undertone--

"I wish to Heaven he'd take a dose of it himself."

And so on from house to house.

I counted up, from one end of the street to the other, that there were living in it seven skunks, fourteen low whelps, eight mean hounds and two dirty skinflints. And all of these merely among the Conservative voters. It made me wish to be a Liberal. Especially as the Liberal voters, by the law of the perversity of human affairs, always seemed to be the finer lot. As they were NOT voting for our candidate, they were able to meet him in a fair and friendly way, whereas William and Jasper and Edward and our "bunch" were always surly and hardly deigned to give more than a growl in answer to the candidate's greeting, without even looking up at him.

But a Liberal voter would stop him in the street and shake hands and say in a frank, cordial way.

"Mr. Grouch, I'm sorry indeed that I can't vote for you, and I'd like to be able to wish you success, but of course you know I'm on the other side and always have been and can't change now."

Whereupon the Candidate would say. "That's all right, John, I don't expect you to. I can respect a man's convictions all right, I guess."

So they would part excellent friends, the Candidate saying as we moved off:

"That man, John Winter, is one of the straightest men in this whole county."

Then he would add--

"Now we'll just go into this house for a minute. There's a dirty pup in here that's one of our supporters."

My opinion of our own supporters went lower every day, and my opinion of the Liberal voters higher, till it so happened that I went one day to an old friend of mine who was working on the Liberal side. I asked him how he liked it.

"Oh, well enough!" he said, "as a sort of game. But in this constituency you've got all the decent voters; our voters are the lowest bunch of skunks I ever struck."

Just then a man passed in a buggy, and looked sourly at my friend the Liberal worker.

"Hullo, John!" he called, with a manufactured hilarity, "got the little mare out for a turn, eh?"

John grunted.

"There's one of them," said my friend, "the lowest pup in this county, John Winter."

"Come along," said the Candidate to me one morning, "I want you to meet my committee."

"You'll find them," he said confidingly, as we started down the street towards the committee rooms, "an awful bunch of mutts."

"Too bad," I said, "what's wrong with them?"

"Oh, I don't know--they're just a pack of simps. They don't seem to have any PUNCH in them. The one you'll meet first is the chairman--he's about the worst dub of the lot; I never saw a man with so little force in my life. He's got no magnetism, that's what's wrong with him--no magnetism."

A few minutes later the Candidate was introducing me to a roomful of heavy looking Committee men. Committee men in politics, I notice, have always a heavy bovine look. They are generally in a sort of daze, or doped from smoking free cigars.

"Now I want to introduce you first," said the Candidate, "to our chairman, Mr. Frog. Mr. Frog is our old battle horse in this constituency. And this is our campaign secretary Mr. Bughouse, and Mr. Dope, and Mr. Mudd, et cetera."

Those may not have been their names.

It is merely what the names sounded like when one was looking into their faces.

The Candidate introduced them all as battle horses, battle axes, battle leaders, standard bearers, flag-holders, and so forth. If he had introduced them as hat-racks or cigar holders, it would have been nearer the mark.

Presently the Candidate went out and I was left with the battle-axes.

"What do you think of our chances?" I asked.

The battle-axes shook their heads with dubious looks.

"Pretty raw deal," said the Chairman, "the Convention wishing HIM on us." He pointed with his thumb over his shoulder to indicate the departed Candidate.

"What's wrong with him?" I asked.

Mr. Frog shook his head again.

"No PUNCH," he said.

"None at all," agreed all the battle horses.

"I'll tell you," said the Campaign secretary, Mr. Bughouse, a voluble man, with wandering eyes--"the trouble is he has no magnetism, no personal magnetism."

"I see," I said.

"Now, you take this man, Shortis, that the Liberals have got hold of," continued Mr. Bughouse, "he's full of MAGNETISM. He appeals."

All the other Committee men nodded.

"That's so," they murmured, "magnetism, Our man hasn't a darned ounce of it."

"I met Shortis the other night in the street," went on Mr. Bughouse, "and he said, 'Come on up to my room in the hotel.' 'Oh,' I said, 'I can't very well.' 'Nonsense,' he said, 'You're on the other side but what does that matter?' Well, we went up to his room, and there he had whiskey, and gin, and lager,--everything. 'Now,' he says, 'name your drink--what is it?' There he was, right in his room, breaking the law without caring a darn about it. Well, you know the voters like that kind of thing. It appeals to them."

"Well," said another of the Committee men,--I think it was the one called Mr. Dope, "I wouldn't mind that so much. But the chief trouble about our man, to my mind, is that he can't speak."

"He can't?" I exclaimed.

All the Committee shook their heads.

"Not for sour apples!" asserted Mr. Dope positively. "Now, in this riding that won't do. Our people here are used to first class speaking, they expect it. I suppose there has been better speaking in this Constituency than anywhere else in the whole dominion. Not lately, perhaps; not in the last few elections. But I can remember, and so can some of the boys here, the election when Sir John A. spoke here, when the old Mackenzie government went out."

He looked around at the circle. Several nodded.

"Remember it as well," assented Mr. Mudd, "as if it were yesterday."

"Well, sir," continued Mr. Dope, "I'll never forget Sir John A. speaking here in the Odd Fellows' Hall, eh?"

The Committee men nodded and gurgled in corroboration.

"My! but he was PLASTERED. We had him over at Pete Robinson's hotel all afternoon, and I tell you he was plastered for fair. We ALL were. I remember I was so pickled myself I could hardly help Sir John up the steps of the platform. So were you, Mudd, do you remember?"

"I certainly was!" said Mr. Mudd proudly. Committee men who would scorn to drink lager beer in 1919, take a great pride, I have observed, in having been pickled in 1878.

"Yes, sir," continued Mr. Dope, "you certainly were pickled. I remember just as well as anything, when they opened the doors and let the crowd in: all the boys had been bowling up and were pretty well soused. You never saw such a crowd. Old Dr. Greenway (boys, you remember the old Doc) was in the chair, and he was pretty well spifflocated. Well, sir, Sir John A. got up in that hall and he made the finest, most moving speech I ever listened to. Do you remember when he called old Trelawney an ash-barrel? And when he made that appeal for a union of hearts and said that the sight of McGuire (the Liberal candidate) made him sick? I tell you those were great days. You don't get speaking like that now; and you don't get audiences like that now either. Not the same calibre."

All the Committee shook their heads.

"Well, anyway, boys," said the Chairman, as he lighted a fresh cigar, "to-morrow will decide, one way or the other. We've certainly worked hard enough,"-- here he passed the box of cigars round to the others--"I haven't been in bed before two any night since the work started."

"Neither have I," said another of the workers. "I was just saying to the wife when I got up this morning that I begin to feel as if I never wanted to see the sight of a card again."

"Well, I don't regret the work," said the Secretary, "so long as we carry the riding. You see," he added in explanation to me, "we're up against a pretty hard proposition here. This riding really is Liberal: they've got the majority of voters though we HAVE once or twice swung it Conservative. But whether we can carry it with a man like Grouch is hard to say. One thing is certain, boys, if he DOES carry it, he doesn't owe it to himself."

All the battle horses agreed on this. A little after that we dispersed.

And twenty-four hours later the vote was taken and to my intense surprise the riding was carried by Grouch the Conservative candidate.

I say, to MY surprise. But apparently not to anybody else.

For it appeared this (was in conversations after the election) that Grouch was a man of extraordinary magnetism. He had, so they said, "punch." Shortis, the Liberal, it seemed, lacked punch absolutely. Even his own supporters admitted that he had no personality whatever. Some wondered how he had the nerve to run.

But my own theory of how the election was carried is quite different.

I feel certain that all the Conservative voters despised their candidate so much that they voted Liberal. And all the Liberals voted Conservative.

That carried the riding.

Meantime Grouch left the constituency by the first train next day for Ottawa. Except for paying taxes on his house, he will not be back in the town till they dissolve parliament again.

5.--The Lost Illusions of Mr. Sims

In the club to which I belong, in a quiet corner where the sunlight falls in sideways, there may be seen sitting of an afternoon my good friend of thirty years' standing, Mr. Edward Sims. Being somewhat afflicted with gout, he generally sits with one foot up on a chair. On a brass table beside him are such things as Mr. Sims needs. But they are few. Wealthy as he is, the needs of Mr. Sims reach scarcely further than Martini cocktails and Egyptian cigarettes. Such poor comforts as these, brought by a deferential waiter, with, let us say, a folded newspaper at five o'clock, suffice for all his wants. Here sits Mr. Sims till the shadows fall in the street outside, when a limousine motor trundles up to the club and rolls him home.

And here of an afternoon Mr. Sims talks to me of his college days when he was young. The last thirty years of his life have moved in so gentle a current upon so smooth a surface that they have been without adventure. It is the stormy period of his youth that preoccupies my friend as he sits looking from the window of the club at the waving leaves in the summer time and the driving snow in the winter.

I am of that habit of mind that makes me prone to listen. And for this, perhaps, Mr. Sims selects me as the recipient of the stories of his college days. It is, it seems, the fixed belief of my good friend that when he was young he belonged at college to a particularly nefarious crowd or group that exists in his mind under the name of the "old gang." The same association, or corporate body or whatever it should be called, is also designated by Mr. Sims, the "old crowd," or more simply and affectionately "the boys." In the recollection of my good friend this "old gang" were of a devilishness since lost off the earth. Work they wouldn't. Sleep they despised. While indoors they played poker in a blue haze of tobacco smoke with beer in jugs and mugs all round them. All night they were out of doors on the sidewalk with linked arms, singing songs in chorus and jeering at the city police.

Yet in spite of life such as this, which might appear to an outsider wearing to the intellect, the "old gang" as recollected by Mr. Sims were of a mental brilliancy that eclipses everything previous or subsequent. McGregor of the Class of '85 graduated with a gold medal in Philosophy after drinking twelve bottles of lager before sitting down to his final examination. Ned Purvis, the football half-back, went straight from the football field after a hard game with his ankle out of joint, drank half a bottle of Bourbon Rye and then wrote an examination in Greek poetry that drew tears from the President of the college.

Mr. Sims is perhaps all the more prone to talk of these early days insomuch that, since his youth, life, in the mere material sense, has used him all too kindly. At an early age, indeed at about the very time of his graduation, Mr. Sims came into money,--not money in the large and frenzied sense of a speculative fortune, begetting care and breeding anxiety, but in the warm and comfortable inheritance of a family brewery, about as old and as well-established as the Constitution of the United States. In this brewery, even to-day, Mr. Sims, I believe, spends a certain part, though no great part, of his time. He is carried to it, I understand, in his limousine in the sunnier hours of the morning; for an hour or so each day he moves about among the warm smell of the barley and the quiet hum of the machinery murmuring among its dust.

There is, too, somewhere in the upper part of the city a huge, silent residence, where a noiseless butler adjusts Mr. Sims's leg on a chair and serves him his dinner in isolated luxury.

But the residence, and the brewery, and with them the current of Mr. Sims's life move of themselves.

Thus has care passed Mr. Sims by, leaving him stranded in a club chair with his heavy foot and stick beside him.

Mr. Sims is a bachelor. Nor is he likely now to marry: but this through no lack of veneration or respect for the sex. It arises, apparently, from the fact that when Mr. Sims was young, during his college days, the beauty and charm of the girls who dwelt in his college town was such as to render all later women mere feeble suggestions of what might have been. There was, as there always is, one girl in particular. I have not heard my friend speak much of her. But I gather that Kate Dashaway was the kind of girl who might have made a fit mate even for the sort of intellectual giant that flourished at Mr. Sims's college. She was not only beautiful. All the girls remembered by Mr. Sims were that. But she was in addition "a good head" and "a good sport," two of the highest qualities that, in Mr. Sims's view, can crown the female sex. She had, he said, no "nonsense" about her, by which term Mr. Sims indicated religion. She drank lager beer, played tennis as well as any man in the college, and smoked cigarettes a whole generation in advance of the age.

Mr. Sims, so I gather, never proposed to her, nor came within a measurable distance of doing so. A man so prone, as is my friend, to spend his time in modest admiration of the prowess of others is apt to lag behind. Miss Dashaway remains to Mr. Sims, as all else does, a retrospect and a regret.

But the chief peculiarities of the old gang--as they exist in the mind of Mr. Sims--is the awful fate that has overwhelmed them. It is not merely that they are scattered to the four corners of the continent. That might have been expected. But, apparently, the most awful moral ruin has fallen upon them. That, at least, is the abiding belief of Mr. Sims.

"Do you ever hear anything of McGregor now?" I ask him sometimes.

"No," he says, shaking his head quietly. "I understand he went all to the devil."

"How was that?"

"Booze," says Mr. Sims. There is a quiet finality about the word that ends all discussion.

"Poor old Curly!" says Mr. Sims, in speaking of another of his classmates. "I guess he's pretty well down and out these days."

"What's the trouble?" I say.

Mr. Sims moves his eyes sideways as he sits. It is easier than moving his head.

"Booze," he says.

Even apparent success in life does not save Mr. Sims's friends.

"I see," I said one day, "that they have just made Arthur Stewart a Chief Justice out west."

"Poor old Artie," murmured Mr. Sims. "He'll have a hard time holding it down. I imagine he's pretty well tanked up all the time these days."

When Mr. Sims has not heard of any of his associates for a certain lapse of years, he decides to himself that they are down and out. It is a form of writing them off. There is a melancholy satisfaction in it. As the years go by Mr. Sims is coming to regard himself and a few others as the lonely survivors of a great flood. All the rest, brilliant as they once were, are presumed to be "boozed," "tanked," "burnt out," "bust-up," and otherwise consumed.

After having heard for so many years the reminiscences of my good friend about the old gang, it seemed almost incredible that one of them should step into actual living being before my eyes. Yet so it happened.

I found Mr. Sims at the club one day, about to lunch there, a thing contrary to his wont. And with him was a friend, a sallow, insignificant man in the middle fifties, with ragged, sandy hair, wearing thin.

"Shake hands with Tommy Vidal," said Mr. Sims proudly.

If he had said, "Shake hands with Aristotle," he couldn't have spoken with greater pride.

This then was Tommy Vidal, the intellectual giant of whom I had heard a hundred times. Tommy had, at college, so Mr. Sims had often assured me, the brightest mind known since the age of Pericles. He took the prize in Latin poetry absolutely "without opening a book." Latin to Tommy Vidal had been, by a kind of natural gift, born in him. In Latin he was "a whale." Indeed in everything. He had passed his graduation examination with first class honours; "plastered." He had to be held in his seat, so it was recorded, while he wrote.

Tommy, it seemed, had just "blown in" to town that morning. It was characteristic of Mr. Sims's idea of the old gang that the only way in which any of them were supposed to enter a town was to "blow in."

"When did you say you 'blew in,' Tommy?" he asked about half a dozen times during our lunch. In reality, the reckless, devil-may-care fellow Vidal had "blown in" to bring his second daughter to a boarding school--a thing no doubt contemplated months ahead. But Mr. Sims insisted in regarding Tommy's movements as purely fortuitous, the sport of chance. He varied his question by asking "When do you expect to 'blow out' Tommy?" Tommy's answers he forgot at once.

We sat and talked after lunch, and it pained me to notice that Tommy Vidal was restless and anxious to get away. Mr. Sims offered him cigars, thick as ropes and black as night, but he refused them. It appeared that he had long since given up smoking. It affected his eyes, he said. The deferential waiter brought brandy and curacoa in long thin glasses. But Mr. Vidal shook his head. He hadn't had a drink, he said, for twenty years. He found it affected his hearing. Coffee, too, he refused. It affected, so it seemed, his sense of smell. He sat beside us, ill at ease, and anxious, as I could see, to get back to his second daughter and her schoolmistresses.

Mr. Sims, who is geniality itself in his heart, but has no great powers in conversation, would ask Tommy if he remembered how he acted as Antigone in the college play, and was "plastered" from the second act on. Mr. Vidal had no recollection of it, but wondered if there was any good book-store in town where he could buy his daughter an Algebra. He rose when he decently could and left us. As Mr. Sims saw it, he "blew out."

Mr. Sims is kindliness itself in his judgments. He passed no word of censure on his departed friend. But a week or so later he mentioned to me in conversation that Tommy Vidal had "turned into a kind of stiff." The vocabulary of Mr. Sims holds no term of deeper condemnation than the word "stiff." To be a "stiff" is the last form of degradation.

It is strange that when a thing happens once, it forthwith happens twice or even more. For years no member of the "old gang" had come in touch with Mr. Sims. Yet the visit of Tommy Vidal was followed at no great distance of time by the "blowing in" of Ned Purvis.

"Well, well!" said Mr. Sims, as he opened one afternoon a telegram that the deferential waiter brought upon a tray. "This beats all! Old Ned Purvis wires that he's going to blow in to town to-night at seven."

Forthwith Mr. Sims fell to ordering dinner for the three of us in a private room, with enough of an assortment of gin cocktails and Scotch highballs to run a distillery, and enough Vichy water and imported soda for a bath. "I know old Ned!" he said as he added item after item to the list.

At seven o'clock the waiter whispered, as in deep confidence, that there was a gentleman below for Mr. Sims.

It so happened that on that evening my friend's foot was in bad shape, and rested on a chair. At his request I went from the lounge room of the club downstairs to welcome the new arrival.

Purvis I knew all about. My friend had spoken of him a thousand times. He had played half-back on the football team--a big hulking brute of a fellow. In fact, he was, as pictured by Mr. Sims, a perfect colossus. And he played football--as did all Mr. Sims's college chums--"plastered." "Old Ned," so Mr. Sims would relate, "was pretty well 'soused' when the game started: but we put a hose at him at half-time and got him into pretty good shape." All men in any keen athletic contest, as remembered by Mr. Sims, were pretty well "tanked up." For the lighter, nimbler games such as tennis, they were reported "spifflocated" and in that shape performed prodigies of agility.

"You'll know Ned," said Mr. Sims, "by his big shoulders." I went downstairs.

The reception room below was empty, except for one man, a little, gentle-looking man with spectacles. He wore black clothes with a waistcoat reaching to the throat, a white tie and a collar buttoned on backwards. Ned Purvis was a clergyman! His great hulking shoulders had gone the way of all my good friend's reminiscences.

I brought him upstairs.

For a moment, in the half light of the room, Mr. Sims was still deceived.

"Well, Ned!" he began heartily, with a struggle to rise from his chair--then he saw the collar and tie of the Rev. Mr. Purvis, and the full horror of the thing dawned upon him. Nor did the three gin cocktails, which Mr. Sims had had stationed ready for the reunion, greatly help its geniality. Yet it had been a maxim, in the recollections of Mr. Sims, that when any of the boys blew in anywhere the bringing of drinks must be instantaneous and uproarious.

Our dinner that night was very quiet.

Mr. Purvis drank only water. That, with a little salad, made his meal. He had a meeting to address that evening at eight, a meeting of women--"dear women" he called them--who had recently affiliated their society with the work that some of the dear women in Mr. Purvis's own town were carrying on. The work, as described, boded no good for breweries. Mr. Purvis's wife, so it seemed, was with him and would also "take the platform."

As best we could we made conversation.

"I didn't know that you were married," said Mr. Sims.

"Yes," said Mr. Purvis, "married, and with five dear boys and three dear girls." The eight of them, he told us, were a great blessing. So, too, was his wife--a great social worker, it seemed, in the cause of women's rights and a marvellous platform speaker in the temperance crusade.

"By the way, Mr. Sims," said Mr. Purvis (they had called one another "Mr." after the first five minutes), "you may remember my wife. I think perhaps you knew her in our college days. She was a Miss Dashaway."

Mr. Sims bowed his head over his plate, as another of his lost illusions vanished into thin air.

After Mr. Purvis had gone, my friend spoke out his mind--once and once only, and more in regret than anger.

"I'm afraid," he said, "that old Ned has turned into a SISSY."

It was only to be expected that the visits of later friends--the "boys" who happened to "blow in"--were disappointments. Art Hamilton, who came next, and who had been one of the most brilliant men of the Class of '86 had turned somehow into a "complete mutt." Jake Todd, who used to write so brilliantly in the college paper, as recollected by Mr. Sims, was now the editor of a big New York daily. Good things might have been expected of him, but it transpired that he had undergone "wizening of the brain." In fact, a number of Mr. Sims's former friends had suffered from this cruel disease, consisting apparently of a shrinkage or contraction of the cerebellum.

Mr. Sims spoke little of his disappointments. But I knew that he thought much about them. They set him wondering. There were changes here that to the thoughtful mind called for investigation.

So I was not surprised when he informed me that it was his intention to visit "the old place" and have a look at it. The "old place," called also the "old shop," indicated, as I knew, Mr. Sims's college, the original scene of the exploits of the old gang. In the thirty years since he had graduated, though separated from it only by two hundred miles, Mr. Sims had never revisited it. So is it always with the most faithful of the sons of learning. The illumination of the inner eye is better than the crude light of reality. College reunions are but for the noisy lip service of the shallow and the interested. The deeper affection glows in the absent heart.

My friend invited me to "come along." We would, he said, "blow in" upon the place and have a look at it.

It was in the fullness of the spring time that we went, when the leaves are out on the college campus, and when Commencement draws near, and when all the college, even the students, are busy.

Mr. Sims, I noted when I joined him at the train, was dressed as for the occasion. He wore a round straw hat with a coloured ribbon, and light grey suit, and a necktie with the garish colours of the college itself. Thus dressed, he leaned as lightly as his foot allowed him upon a yellow stick, and dreamed himself again an undergraduate.

I had thought the purpose of his visit a mere curiosity bred in his disappointment. It appeared that I was wrong. On the train Mr. Sims unfolded to me that his idea in "blowing in" upon his college was one of benefaction. He had it in his mind, he said, to do something for the "old place," no less a thing than to endow a chair. He explained to me, modestly as was his wont, the origin of his idea. The brewing business, it appeared, was rapidly reaching a stage when it would have to be wound up. The movement of prohibition would necessitate, said Mr. Sims, the closing of the plant. The prospect, in the financial sense, occasioned my friend but little excitement. I was given to understand that prohibition, in the case of Mr. Sims's brewery, had long since been "written off" or "written up" or at least written somewhere where it didn't matter. And the movement itself Mr. Sims does not regard as permanent. Prohibition, he says, is bound to be washed out by a "turn of the tide"; in fact, he speaks of this returning wave of moral regeneration much as Martin Luther might have spoken of the Protestant Reformation. But for the time being the brewery will close. Mr. Sims had thought deeply, it seemed, about putting his surplus funds into the manufacture of commercial alcohol, itself a noble profession. For some time his mind has wavered between that and endowing a chair of philosophy. There is, and always has been, a sort of natural connection between the drinking of beer and deep quiet thought. Mr. Sims, as a brewer, felt that philosophy was the proper thing.

We left the train, walked through the little town and entered the university gates.

"Gee!" said Mr. Sims, pausing a moment and leaning on his stick, "were the gates only as big as that?"

We began to walk up the avenue.

"I thought there were more trees to it than these," said Mr. Sims.

"Yes," I answered. "You often said that the avenue was a quarter of a mile long."

"So the thing used to be," he murmured.

Then Mr. Sims looked at the campus. "A dinky looking little spot," he said.

"Didn't you say," I asked, "that the Arts Building was built of white marble?"

"Always thought it was," he answered. "Looks like rough cast from here, doesn't it."

"We'll have to go in and see the President, I suppose," continued Mr. Sims. He said it with regret. Something of his undergraduate soul had returned to his body. Although he had never seen the President (this one) in his life, and had only read of his appointment some five years before in the newspapers, Mr. Sims was afraid of him.

"Now, I tell you," he went on. "We'll just make a break in and then a quick get-away. Don't let's get anchored in there, see? If the old fellow gets talking, he'll go on for ever. I remember the way it used to be when a fellow had to go in to see Prexy in my time. The old guy would start mooning away and quoting Latin and keep us there half the morning."

At this moment two shabby-looking, insignificant men who had evidently come out from one of the buildings, passed us on the sidewalk.

"I wonder who those guys are," said Mr. Sims. "Look like bums, don't they?"

I shook my head. Some instinct told me that they were professors. But I didn't say so.

My friend continued his instructions.

"When the President asks us to lunch," he said, "I'll say that we're lunching with a friend down town, see? Then we'll make a break and get out. If he says he wants to introduce us to the Faculty or anything like that, then you say that we have to get the twelve-thirty to New York, see? I'm not going to say anything about a chair in philosophy to-day. I want to read it up first some night so as to be able to talk about it."

To all of this I agreed.

From a janitor we inquired where to find the President.

"In the Administration Building, eh?" said Mr. Sims. "That's a new one on me. The building on the right, eh? Thank you."

"See the President?" said a young lady in an ante-office. "I'm not sure whether you can see him just now. Have you an appointment?"

Mr. Sims drew out a card. "Give him that" he said. On the card he had scribbled "Graduate of 1887."

In a few minutes we were shown into another room where there was a young man, evidently the President's secretary, and a number of people waiting.

"Will you kindly sit down," murmured the young man, in a consulting-room voice, "and wait? The President is engaged just now."

We waited. Through the inner door leading to the President people went and came. Mr. Sims, speaking in whispers, continued to caution me on the quickness of our get-away.

Presently the young man touched him on the shoulder.

"The President will see you now," he whispered.

We entered the room. The "old guy" rose to meet us, Mr. Sims's card in his hand. But he was not old. He was at least ten years younger than either of us. He was, in fact, what Mr. Sims and I would almost have called a boy. In dress and manner he looked as spruce and busy as the sales manager of a shoe factory.

"Delighted to see you, gentlemen," he said, shaking hands effusively. "We are always pleased to see our old graduates, Mr. Samson--No, I beg pardon, Mr. Sims--class of '97, I see--No, I beg your pardon, Class of '67, I read it wrongly--"

I heard Mr. Sims murmuring something that seemed to contain the words "a look around."

"Yes, yes, exactly," said the President. "A look round, you'll find a great deal to interest you in looking about the place, I'm sure, Mr. Samson, great changes. I'm extremely sorry I can't offer to take you round myself," here he snapped a gold watch open and shut, "the truth is I have to catch the twelve-thirty to New York--so sorry."

Then he shook our hands again, very warmly.

In another moment we were outside the door. The get-away was accomplished.

We walked out of the building and towards the avenue.

As we passed the portals of the Arts Building, a noisy, rackety crowd of boys--evidently, to our eyes, schoolboys --came out, jostling and shouting. They swarmed past us, accidentally, no doubt, body-checking Mr. Sims, whose straw hat was knocked off and rolled on the sidewalk. A janitor picked it up for him as the crowd of boys passed.

"What pack of young bums are those?" asked Mr. Sims. "You oughtn't to let young roughs like that come into the buildings. Are they here from some school or something?"

"No sir," said the janitor. "They're students."

"Students?" repeated Mr. Sims. "And what are they shouting like that for?"

"There's a notice up that their professor is ill, and so the class is cancelled, sir."

"Class!" said Mr. Sims. "Are those a class?"

"Yes, sir," said the janitor. "That's the Senior Class in Philosophy."

Mr. Sims said nothing. He seemed to limp more than his custom as we passed down the avenue.

On the way home on the train he talked much of crude alcohol and the possibilities of its commercial manufacture.

So far as I know, his only benefaction up to date has been the two dollars that he gave to a hackman to drive us away from the college.

6.--Fetching the Doctor: From Recollections of
Childhood in the Canadian Countryside

We lived far back in the country, such as it used to be in Canada, before the days of telephones and motor cars, with long lonely roads and snake fences buried in deep snow, and with cedar swamps where the sleighs could hardly pass two abreast. Here and there, on a winter night, one saw the light in a farm house, distant and dim.

Over it all was a great silence such as people who live in the cities can never know.

And on us, as on the other families of that lonely countryside, there sometimes fell the sudden alarm of illness, and the hurrying drive through the snow at night to fetch the doctor from the village, seven miles away.

My elder brother and I--there was a long tribe of us, as with all country families--would hitch up the horse by the light of the stable lantern, eager with haste and sick with fear, counting the time till the doctor could be there.

Then out into the driving snow, urging the horse that knew by instinct that something was amiss, and so mile after mile, till we rounded the corner into the single street of the silent village.

Late, late at night it was--eleven o'clock, perhaps--and the village dark and deep in sleep, except where the light showed red against the blinds of the "Surgery" of the doctor's rough-cast house behind the spruce trees.

"Doctor," we cried, as we burst in, "hurry and come. Jim's ill--"

I can see him still as he sat there in his surgery, the burly doctor, rugged and strong for all the sixty winters that he carried. There he sat playing chess--always he seemed to be playing chess--with his son, a medical student, burly and rugged already as himself.

"Shut the door, shut the door!" he called. "Come in, boys; here, let me brush that snow off you--it's my move Charlie, remember--now, what the devil's the matter?"

Then we would pant out our hurried exclamations, both together.

"Bah!" he growled, "ill nothing! Mere belly ache, I guess."

That was his term, his favorite word, for an undiagnosed disease--"belly ache." They call it supergastral aesthesia now. In a city house, it sounds better. Yet how we hung upon the doctor's good old Saxon term, yearning and hoping that it might be that.

But even as he growled the doctor had taken down a lantern from a hook, thrown on a huge, battered fur coat that doubled his size, and was putting medicines--a very shopful it seemed--into a leather case.

"Your horse is done up," he said. "We'll put my mare in. Come and give me a hand, Charlie."

He was his own hostler and stable-man, he and his burly son. Yet how quickly and quietly he moved, the lantern swinging on his arm, as he buckled the straps. "What kind of a damn fool tug is this you've got?" he would say.

Then, in a moment, as it seemed, out into the wind and snow again, the great figure of the doctor almost filling the seat of the cutter, the two of us crushed in beside him, with responsibility, the unbearable burden, gone from us, and renewed comfort in our hearts.

Little is said on the way: our heads are bent against the storm: the long stride of the doctor's mare eats up the flying road.

Then as we near the farm house and see the light in the sick-room window, fear clutches our hearts again.

"You boys unhitch," says the doctor. "I'll go right in."

Presently, when we enter the house, we find that he is in the sick-room--the door closed. No word of comfort has come forth. He has sent out for hot blankets. The stoves are to be kept burning. We must sit up. We may be needed. That is all.

And there in that still room through the long night, he fights single-handed against Death. Behind him is no human help, no consultation, no wisdom of the colleges to call in; only his own unaided strength, and his own firm purpose and that strange instinct in the fight for a flickering life, that some higher power than that of colleges has planted deep within his soul.

So we watch through the night hours, in dull misery and fear, a phantom at the window pane: so must we wait till the slow morning shows dim and pale at the windows.

Then he comes out from the room. His face is furrowed with the fatigue of his long vigil. But as he speaks the tone of his voice is as that of one who has fought and conquered.

"There--he'll do now. Give him this when he wakes."

Then a great joy sweeps over us as the phantom flees away, and we shudder back into the warm sunshine of life, while the sound of the doctor's retreating sleighbells makes music to our ears.

And once it was not so. The morning dawned and he did not come from the darkened room: only there came to our listening ears at times the sound of a sob or moan, and the doctor's voice, firm and low, but with all hope gone from it.

And when at last he came, his face seemed old and sad as we had never seen it. He paused a moment on the threshold and we heard him say, "I have done all that I can." Then he beckoned us into the darkened room, and, for the first time, we knew Death.

All that is forty years ago.

They tell me that, since then, the practice of medicine has been vastly improved. There are specialists now, I understand, for every conceivable illness and for every subdivision of it. If I fall ill, there is a whole battery of modern science to be turned upon me in a moment. There are X-rays ready to penetrate me in all directions. I may have any and every treatment--hypnotic, therapeutic or thaumaturgic--for which I am able to pay.

But, oh, my friends, when it shall come to be my lot to be ill and stricken--in the last and real sense, with the Great Fear upon me, and the Dark Phantom at the pane--then let some one go, fast and eager--though it be only in the paths of an expiring memory--fast and eager, through the driving snow to bring him to my bedside. Let me hear the sound of his hurrying sleighbells as he comes, and his strong voice without the door--and, if that may not be, then let me seem at least to feel the clasp of his firm hand to guide me without fear to the Land of Shadows, where he has gone before.

The Codes Of Hammurabi And Moses
W. W. Davies

QTY

The discovery of the Hammurabi Code is one of the greatest achievements of archaeology, and is of paramount interest, not only to the student of the Bible, but also to all those interested in ancient history...

Religion   **ISBN:** *1-59462-338-4*   **Pages:132**
MSRP $12.95

The Theory of Moral Sentiments
Adam Smith

QTY

This work from 1749. contains original theories of conscience amd moral judgment and it is the foundation for systemof morals.

Philosophy   **ISBN:** *1-59462-777-0*   **Pages:536**
MSRP $19.95

Jessica's First Prayer
Hesba Stretton

QTY

In a screened and secluded corner of one of the many railway-bridges which span the streets of London there could be seen a few years ago, from five o'clock every morning until half past eight, a tidily set-out coffee-stall, consisting of a trestle and board, upon which stood two large tin cans, with a small fire of charcoal burning under each so as to keep the coffee boiling during the early hours of the morning when the work-people were thronging into the city on their way to their daily toil...

Pages:84

Childrens   **ISBN:** *1-59462-373-2*   *MSRP $9.95*

My Life and Work
Henry Ford

QTY

Henry Ford revolutionized the world with his implementation of mass production for the Model T automobile. Gain valuable business insight into his life and work with his own auto-biography... "We have only started on our development of our country we have not as yet, with all our talk of wonderful progress, done more than scratch the surface. The progress has been wonderful enough but..."

Pages:300

Biographies/   **ISBN:** *1-59462-198-5*   *MSRP $21.95*

The Art of Cross-Examination
Francis Wellman

QTY

I presume it is the experience of every author, after his first book is published upon an important subject, to be almost overwhelmed with a wealth of ideas and illustrations which could readily have been included in his book, and which to his own mind, at least, seem to make a second edition inevitable. Such certainly was the case with me; and when the first edition had reached its sixth impression in five months, I rejoiced to learn that it seemed to my publishers that the book had met with a sufficiently favorable reception to justify a second and considerably enlarged edition. ...

Pages:412

Reference   **ISBN: *1-59462-647-2***   *MSRP $19.95*

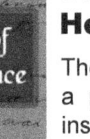

On the Duty of Civil Disobedience
Henry David Thoreau

QTY

Thoreau wrote his famous essay, On the Duty of Civil Disobedience, as a protest against an unjust but popular war and the immoral but popular institution of slave-owning. He did more than write—he declined to pay his taxes, and was hauled off to gaol in consequence. Who can say how much this refusal of his hastened the end of the war and of slavery ?

Law   **ISBN: *1-59462-747-9***   **Pages:48**

MSRP $7.45

Dream Psychology
Psychoanalysis for Beginners

Sigmund Freud

Dream Psychology Psychoanalysis for Beginners
Sigmund Freud

QTY

Sigmund Freud, born Sigismund Schlomo Freud (May 6, 1856 - September 23, 1939), was a Jewish-Austrian neurologist and psychiatrist who co-founded the psychoanalytic school of psychology. Freud is best known for his theories of the unconscious mind, especially involving the mechanism of repression; his redefinition of sexual desire as mobile and directed towards a wide variety of objects; and his therapeutic techniques, especially his understanding of transference in the therapeutic relationship and the presumed value of dreams as sources of insight into unconscious desires.

Pages:196

Psychology   **ISBN: *1-59462-905-6***   *MSRP $15.45*

The Miracle of Right Thought
Orison Swett Marden

QTY

Believe with all of your heart that you will do what you were made to do. When the mind has once formed the habit of holding cheerful, happy, prosperous pictures, it will not be easy to form the opposite habit. It does not matter how improbable or how far away this realization may see, or how dark the prospects may be, if we visualize them as best we can, as vividly as possible, hold tenaciously to them and vigorously struggle to attain them, they will gradually become actualized, realized in the life. But a desire, a longing without endeavor, a yearning abandoned or held indifferently will vanish without realization.

Pages:360

Self Help   **ISBN: *1-59462-644-8***   *MSRP $25.45*

The Rosicrucian Cosmo-Conception Mystic Christianity *by Max Heindel*   ISBN: *1-59462-188-8* **$38.95**
The Rosicrucian Cosmo-conception is not dogmatic, neither does it appeal to any other authority than the reason of the student. It is: not controversial, but is: sent forth in the, hope that it may help to clear...   *New Age/Religion Pages 646*

Abandonment To Divine Providence *by Jean-Pierre de Caussade*   ISBN: *1-59462-228-0* **$25.95**
"The Rev. Jean Pierre de Caussade was one of the most remarkable spiritual writers of the Society of Jesus in France in the 18th Century. His death took place at Toulouse in 1751. His works have gone through many editions and have been republished...   *Inspirational/Religion Pages 400*

Mental Chemistry *by Charles Haanel*   ISBN: *1-59462-192-6* **$23.95**
Mental Chemistry allows the change of material conditions by combining and appropriately utilizing the power of the mind. Much like applied chemistry creates something new and unique out of careful combinations of chemicals the mastery of mental chemistry...   *New Age Pages 354*

The Letters of Robert Browning and Elizabeth Barret Barrett 1845-1846 vol II   ISBN: *1-59462-193-4* **$35.95**
by Robert Browning and Elizabeth Barrett   *Biographies Pages 596*

Gleanings In Genesis (volume I) *by Arthur W. Pink*   ISBN: *1-59462-130-6* **$27.45**
Appropriately has Genesis been termed "the seed plot of the Bible" for in it we have, in germ form, almost all of the great doctrines which are afterwards fully developed in the books of Scripture which follow...   *Religion/Inspirational Pages 420*

The Master Key *by L. W. de Laurence*   ISBN: *1-59462-001-6* **$30.95**
In no branch of human knowledge has there been a more lively increase of the spirit of research during the past few years than in the study of Psychology, Concentration and Mental Discipline. The requests for authentic lessons in Thought Control, Mental Discipline and...   *New Age/Business Pages 422*

The Lesser Key Of Solomon Goetia *by L. W. de Laurence*   ISBN: *1-59462-092-X* **$9.95**
This translation of the first book of the "Lernegton" which is now for the first time made accessible to students of Talismanic Magic was done, after careful collation and edition, from numerous Ancient Manuscripts in Hebrew, Latin, and French...   *New Age/Occult Pages 92*

Rubaiyat Of Omar Khayyam *by Edward Fitzgerald*   ISBN: *1-59462-332-5* **$13.95**
Edward Fitzgerald, whom the world has already learned, in spite of his own efforts to remain within the shadow of anonymity, to look upon as one of the rarest poets of the century, was born at Bredfield, in Suffolk, on the 31st of March, 1809. He was the third son of John Purcell...   *Music Pages 172*

Ancient Law *by Henry Maine*   ISBN: *1-59462-128-4* **$29.95**
The chief object of the following pages is to indicate some of the earliest ideas of mankind, as they are reflected in Ancient Law, and to point out the relation of those ideas to modern thought.   *Religiom/History Pages 452*

Far-Away Stories *by William J. Locke*   ISBN: *1-59462-129-2* **$19.45**
"Good wine needs no bush, but a collection of mixed vintages does. And this book is just such a collection. Some of the stories I do not want to remain buried for ever in the museum files of dead magazine-numbers an author's not unpardonable vanity..."   *Fiction Pages 272*

Life of David Crockett *by David Crockett*   ISBN: *1-59462-250-7* **$27.45**
"Colonel David Crockett was one of the most remarkable men of the times in which he lived. Born in humble life, but gifted with a strong will, an indomitable courage, and unremitting perseverance...   *Biographies/New Age Pages 424*

Lip-Reading *by Edward Nitchie*   ISBN: *1-59462-206-X* **$25.95**
Edward B. Nitchie, founder of the New York School for the Hard of Hearing, now the Nitchie School of Lip-Reading, Inc, wrote "LIP-READING Principles and Practice". The development and perfecting of this meritorious work on lip-reading was an undertaking...   *How-to Pages 400*

A Handbook of Suggestive Therapeutics, Applied Hypnotism, Psychic Science   ISBN: *1-59462-214-0* **$24.95**
by Henry Munro   *Health/New Age/Health/Self-help Pages 376*

A Doll's House: and Two Other Plays *by Henrik Ibsen*   ISBN: *1-59462-112-8* **$19.95**
Henrik Ibsen created this classic when in revolutionary 1848 Rome. Introducing some striking concepts in playwriting for the realist genre, this play has been studied the world over.   *Fiction/Classics/Plays 308*

The Light of Asia *by sir Edwin Arnold*   ISBN: *1-59462-204-3* **$13.95**
In this poetic masterpiece, Edwin Arnold describes the life and teachings of Buddha. The man who was to become known as Buddha to the world was born as Prince Gautama of India but he rejected the worldly riches and abandoned the reigns of power when...   *Religion/History/Biographies Pages 170*

The Complete Works of Guy de Maupassant *by Guy de Maupassant*   ISBN: *1-59462-157-8* **$16.95**
"For days and days, nights and nights, I had dreamed of that first kiss which was to consecrate our engagement, and I knew not on what spot I should put my lips..."   *Fiction/Classics Pages 240*

The Art of Cross-Examination *by Francis L. Wellman*   ISBN: *1-59462-309-0* **$26.95**
Written by a renowned trial lawyer, Wellman imparts his experience and uses case studies to explain how to use psychology to extract desired information through questioning.   *How-to/Science/Reference Pages 408*

Answered or Unanswered? *by Louisa Vaughan*   ISBN: *1-59462-248-5* **$10.95**
Miracles of Faith in China   *Religion Pages 112*

The Edinburgh Lectures on Mental Science (1909) *by Thomas*   ISBN: *1-59462-008-3* **$11.95**
This book contains the substance of a course of lectures recently given by the writer in the Queen Street Hall, Edinburgh. Its purpose is to indicate the Natural Principles governing the relation between Mental Action and Material Conditions...   *New Age/Psychology Pages 148*

Ayesha *by H. Rider Haggard*   ISBN: *1-59462-301-5* **$24.95**
Verily and indeed it is the unexpected that happens! Probably if there was one person upon the earth from whom the Editor of this, and of a certain previous history, did not expect to hear again...   *Classics Pages 380*

Ayala's Angel *by Anthony Trollope*   ISBN: *1-59462-352-X* **$29.95**
The two girls were both pretty, but Lucy who was twenty-one who supposed to be simple and comparatively unattractive, whereas Ayala was credited, as her Bombwhat romantic name might show, with poetic charm and a taste for romance. Ayala when her father died was nineteen...   *Fiction Pages 484*

The American Commonwealth *by James Bryce*   ISBN: *1-59462-286-8* **$34.45**
An interpretation of American democratic political theory. It examines political mechanics and society from the perspective of Scotsman James Bryce   *Politics Pages 572*

Stories of the Pilgrims *by Margaret P. Pumphrey*   ISBN: *1-59462-116-0* **$17.95**
This book explores pilgrims religious oppression in England as well as their escape to Holland and eventual crossing to America on the Mayflower, and their early days in New England...   *History Pages 268*

www.bookjungle.com *email: sales@bookjungle.com fax: 630-214-0564 mail: Book Jungle PO Box 2226 Champaign, IL 61825*

QTY

The Fasting Cure *by Sinclair Upton*   ISBN: *1-59462-222-1*   **$13.95**
In the Cosmopolitan Magazine for May, 1910, and in the Contemporary Review (London) for April, 1910, I published an article dealing with my experiences in fasting. I have written a great many magazine articles, but never one which attracted so much attention... New Age/Self Help/Health Pages 164

Hebrew Astrology *by Sepharial*   ISBN: *1-59462-308-2*   **$13.45**
In these days of advanced thinking it is a matter of common observation that we have left many of the old landmarks behind and that we are now pressing forward to greater heights and to a wider horizon than that which represented the mind-content of our progenitors...   Astrology Pages 144

Thought Vibration or The Law of Attraction in the Thought World   ISBN: *1-59462-127-6*   **$12.95**

by William Walker Atkinson   *Psychology/Religion Pages 144*

Optimism *by Helen Keller*   ISBN: *1-59462-108-X*   **$15.95**
Helen Keller was blind, deaf, and mute since 19 months old, yet famously learned how to overcome these handicaps, communicate with the world, and spread her lectures promoting optimism.   An inspiring read for everyone...   Biographies/Inspirational Pages 84

Sara Crewe *by Frances Burnett*   ISBN: *1-59462-360-0*   **$9.45**
In the first place, Miss Minchin lived in London. Her home was a large, dull, tall one, in a large, dull square, where all the houses were alike, and all the sparrows were alike, and where all the door-knockers made the same heavy sound...   Childrens/Classic Pages 88

The Autobiography of Benjamin Franklin *by Benjamin Franklin*   ISBN: *1-59462-135-7*   **$24.95**
The Autobiography of Benjamin Franklin has probably been more extensively read than any other American historical work, and no other book of its kind has had such ups and downs of fortune. Franklin lived for many years in England, where he was agent...   Biographies/History Pages 332

Name	
Email	
Telephone	
Address	
City, State ZIP	

☐ **Credit Card**   ☐ **Check / Money Order**

Credit Card Number	
Expiration Date	
Signature	

Please Mail to: Book Jungle
PO Box 2226
Champaign, IL 61825
or Fax to: 630-214-0564

ORDERING INFORMATION

web: *www.bookjungle.com*
email: *sales@bookjungle.com*
fax: *630-214-0564*
mail: *Book Jungle PO Box 2226 Champaign, IL 61825*
or PayPal *to sales@bookjungle.com*

Please contact us for bulk discounts

DIRECT-ORDER TERMS

**20% Discount if You Order
Two or More Books**
Free Domestic Shipping!
Accepted: Master Card, Visa,
Discover, American Express